ROGUE YOU LIKE A HURRICANE

Rogues of Redemption, Book 2

BY

BRENNA ASH

ARE YOU SIGNED UP FOR DRAGONBLADE'S BLOG?

You'll get the latest news and information on exclusive giveaways, exclusive excerpts, coming releases, sales, free books, cover reveals and more.

Check out our complete list of authors, too!

No spam, no junk. That's a promise!

Sign Up Here

www.dragonbladepublishing.com

Dearest Reader;

Thank you for your support of a small press. At Dragonblade Publishing, we strive to bring you the highest quality Historical Romance from some of the best authors in the business. Without your support, there is no 'us', so we sincerely hope you adore these stories and find some new favorite authors along the way.

Happy Reading!

CEO, Dragonblade Publishing

ADDITIONAL DRAGONBLADE BOOKS BY AUTHOR BRENNA ASH

Rogues of Redemption Series
Sweet Rogue O' Mine (Book 1)
Rogue You Like a Hurricane (Book 2)

CHAPTER ONE

Huntly Castle, 1815

ALEXANDER CAMPBELL, DUKE of Argyll had not visited Huntly Castle, the ancestral home of his best friend, Nicholas Gordon, in years. Not since he'd left to serve his time in the Peninsular War. Something he'd done as his duty to the country, but also something he was glad was now over. While his station afforded him the high position of general, there were many others that fought alongside him that held no such privilege. Together, they'd witnessed atrocities that no one should be subjected to.

As his carriage bumped along the cobblestone path that would lead Alexander to the front entrance of the castle, his body jarred from side to side. It hadn't been a smooth journey from his own castle, Millwool, in Inveraray. For two days, rocky roads caused the carriage to shift roughly, jostling him about. His arse was sore, and he was looking forward to escaping the suppression of the cabin. The walls seemed to be closing in on him. The air was stifling, and he loosened the knot of his cravat, so it didn't feel so restrictive.

He would be much happier if he was riding his horse with the fresh air caressing his skin instead of sitting inside this box. But he had to make a proper appearance and while the Berline offered more space than what he needed just for himself, it was the best he had to endure the journey from Inveraray to Huntly. It had been two long, trying days and he was glad to be seeing the tail end of the ride. His patience had evaporated outside of Braemar, when they'd had to stop and replace one of the wheels.

A sharp knock on the carriage wall followed by, "We shall be arriving shortly, Your Grace," had Alexander sitting up straight. The need to stretch his legs called to him.

The upcoming week would be spent catching up with friends who were all gathering to celebrate Nicholas's return. More than certain a demand of his meddling mother. God bless her. She only wanted what was best for her son, but Hell would freeze over before Nicholas hosted his own return party. Ofttimes, his friend just wanted to be left alone.

The carriage ground to a halt, causing Alexander to jerk in his seat. The footman opened the door, the dust of the road kicked up by the horses settling around them. Stepping out, he paused, taking in the castle's facade. The forbidding grayish-brown stone always a direct contrast to the cheerfulness of the inside, filled with light and love. It would be hard to be anything but with the seven Gordon siblings inside.

Alexander hadn't the faintest idea how Nicholas dealt with his six brothers and sisters, especially the younger ones, a set of ten-year old twins that brimmed with energy. He only had his twenty-two-year-old younger brother, Christopher, to deal with and that one sibling was almost more than he could handle.

He didn't want to think about the mess of the estate finances Christopher had created while Alexander was away.

"Campbell," Nicholas bellowed from the arched doorway.

Alexander grinned, all thoughts of Christopher pushed from his mind as he closed the distance. "Brother, how do ye fare?" he asked Nicholas. Not brothers by blood, but they'd spent so much time growing up together, they might as well have been.

"I am well. Though I must confess my mother has been quite busy." He rolled his eyes at the mention of the Gordon matriarch.

They clasped hands and smacked each other on the back. "Aye, seems so," Alexander chuckled and followed Nicholas inside, greeting Reginald, the Gordon family butler as he passed.

"I've heard mumblings about an engagement?"

They rounded the corner and turned down the hall that would lead them to the study.

Nicholas huffed. "Och. I dinna want to speak of it. She has…"

Up ahead, a vision sent from heaven above stood there. Alexander hadn't seen her in a few years.

Clarissa Gordon. Nicholas's sister.

Nicholas's voice faded into the background as he continued to talk.

The years had been kind. Very kind. She'd grown into a stunning beauty. Her black hair was curled and piled high on top of her head, showing off her slim neckline, which was only accentuated by her ample bosom. His body roared to life, and he shifted slightly. Unable to tear his eyes away.

When their gazes clashed together, Clarissa's brown eyes rounded, her lips parting, before she clamped her mouth shut and grabbed the lass she was with, tugging her along as they went in the opposite direction and disappeared out the door.

"Alexander?" Nicholas questioned. "Ye all right?"

Alexander nodded, but nay, he was most definitely not as he stiffly followed Nicholas into the study and grimaced as he took a seat in one of the leather chairs.

Nicholas filled two glasses with whisky and handed him one. Accepting it, he tried to tamp down the groan that threatened to escape him.

Clarissa was Nicholas's sister. His best friend's *younger* sister. Nicholas would never allow it and rightfully so. His reputation with the lasses was known far and wide and commitment wasn't something he could comprehend.

But the vision of the lass was seared into his memory, and no amount of whisky would wash that away.

CHAPTER TWO

Millwool Castle, Six months later

ALEXANDER CAMPBELL CRADLED his head in his hands, irritation coursing through his veins like wildfire. The cause was none other than his younger brother.

Christopher sat across from him, slumped in a chair, fidgeting nervously while his eyes bounced around the Duke of Argyll's study.

"All of them are gone?" Alexander questioned, his voice ominously quiet. He was referring to their flock of sheep. Prize-winning sheep. Sheep that produced the finest wool which kept them fed and their holdings secure.

"Aye."

"Shite!" Alexander cursed. "Are ye daft? What the hell were ye thinking?"

Christopher flinched, his face pale as he straightened. "I didna mean for things to take such a turn. I was doing verra well—until I wasna."

"I kenned I should have hired someone to watch over the books while I was away." Alexander stood, pushing away from his desk, the chair legs scraped angrily along the polished floorboards, and braced his hands on the desktop, glaring at his brother. "Ye are out of control. Your carelessness has put Millwool in a precarious position."

But he wasn't only angry at his brother; this was partially his fault. His brother had naught interest in running the estate, and as had now been proven, naught knowledge in it, as well.

"I ken. I will fix it."

Alexander barked out a laugh. "Pray tell how ye will do such a thing?" He jabbed a finger in his brother's direction. "And dinna ye daresay ye will win it back at cards. Your subpar game skills are the cause of this current predicament in which we find ourselves in."

"I just need two, mayhap three, well-played hands at the tables and the flock will be back in Campbell hands." Christopher sounded as though he actually believed what he was saying.

"Och, nay. If ye think I am going to stand by and allow ye to gamble Millwool's future away, ye are more daft than I originally believed." He shook his head in disbelief. "I wasna e'en gone verra long. No' this time. 'Twas one thing when ye managed to ruin our estates finances while I was off serving. But hell's teeth, brother, I was gone but a fortnight, and ye managed to lose our livelihood?" Alexander pushed his hands through his hair. He wanted to throttle his brother. Make him understand the dire consequences he had put them in. Instead, he poured himself a whisky and drank deep, letting the smooth burn as it wound its way down his throat try to calm his nerves. But it failed to quell his anger. Maniacal laughter burst from Alexander. "I dinna ken how ye could have been so careless."

The statement was only partially true. Their finances were a mess. Christopher lacked the maturity and knowledge to run a household. It was going to take months to repair the damage he'd done. But losing the sheep? That was the hardest thing to take.

Where were the sheep now? Were they being well-tended? He only cared about their safety. Aye, they were animals, but Alexander cared for them, nonetheless. He, like their father, had always treated them well. Had raised the wee lambs from birth. That flock was the means behind their successful family.

And now they were gone.

"Brother. Ye're overreacting." The words hung in the air, but there was no fight behind them.

Christopher stood, and Alexander studied him, taking in the tired creases around his eyes. The way his shoulders slumped in defeat. His unkempt brown hair standing out in all directions.

With a sigh, he addressed his brother. The urge to beat some sense into him lessened. He could tell Christopher was punishing himself more than Alexander ever could. "Go get washed up and get some sleep." He jerked his head towards the door. "Ye look like hell. When ye're rested, we can discuss our plan for reacquiring our flock."

He watched Christopher amble out of the study and pushed his hands through his hair once again before pouring himself another whisky and emptied the glass in one sip, hissing as it burned his chest. His brother had made a dire mess of things and depending on whom he'd lost the sheep to determined how difficult it would be to regain them.

Alexander only hoped that luck would be on their side, and it wouldn't prove to be as challenging as he expected.

But above all, his biggest worry was there was no guarantee that the flock was being cared for as they required. He hoped they had some type of shelter to allow them to get out of the elements if needed. Was the area where they were being held safe from predators? Worse yet, he prayed they had not been sheared. Lord, he hoped no'. He didn't want anyone making money off of Campbell wool that wasn't a Campbell. Especially someone that didn't deserve to have his sheep in the first place.

Setting the glass down on his desk, his eyes grazed the books that showed every poor choice his brother had made for Millwool while he'd been gone. They had a long road ahead of them to clean up his mess, but the most important thing was to regain possession of their sheep.

He had some money stored away, thankfully in a place his brother hadn't thought of looking or he feared he would have lost that money as well. Alexander only hoped it would be enough to pay off his brother's debts so he could bring the flock back home. His sheep weren't the only thing he had to worry about.

Tomorrow, Nicholas Gordon would be arriving, along with his wife, Gwen, and his younger sister, Clarissa, for their planned visit. It had been a few months since their wedding. It was the last time they had seen each other, and Nicholas had recently sent word that he and Gwen would like to visit for some time. It was only later that he learned that Clarissa would be accompanying them. His body flared to life at the thought of his best friend's sister. She'd blossomed into a stunning woman while they were away at war fighting for their country. He hadn't believed his eyes when he'd seen her when he'd first visited Huntly after his return. Her dark brown hair long and flowing, her doe like brown eyes rich as the drinking chocolate he'd consumed in France.

Unable to spend any meaningful time with her on his initial visit to her home, he was able to spend a bit more time with her at Nicholas and Gwen's wedding. But not enough to satisfy his liking and he hoped to rectify that while she stayed at Millwool.

Nicholas had already warned her against him. He had also told Alexander to stay away from his sister. He wasn't sure how he felt about that. Aye, his friend knew him better than anyone else. He'd had more than his fair share of the lassies, and his bed had never been lonely. Until he'd seen Clarissa. She had blossomed into a beautiful woman, and he had been enraptured. Ever since then, he couldn't help but notice and admire her, the other lasses failing to capture his attention the way they once did. He had tried. Lord had he tried. But losing himself in a woman did not hold quite the same appeal as before.

But Nicholas didn't know that. If Alexander had a sister, he would also warn her against someone like him. A man who approached women for one purpose, a man averse to commitment. He only had his father to blame for that mindset. As the man had always said, why settle down with one lass, when you could have a never-ending stream of them? That way one never got bored by being committed to one woman.

Alexander didn't want to be bored. He had seen how boredom overtook his father and how loathsome he began to feel towards his mother. He never wanted to feel that way with a woman. It was easier to keep his freedom. And his heart. No one could break it if he didn't allow them to have it.

And yet, there was Clarissa, consuming his every thought.

The image of her seared his eyelids at night when he went to bed, falling asleep to the memory of her soft laughter.

The timing could not be worse for their visit, though. He would have to divide his time between playing host and trying to recover his lost flock of sheep. "Och, bloody hell," he cursed to himself and walked from the study. He had things far more important to do. Things that his livelihood, not just his, but everyone he was responsible for, were dependent on. The last thing he needed was the distraction of a beautiful lass keeping his mind occupied on anything but the business at hand.

"GOOD MORN, BROTHER," Christopher stated as he entered the sunroom where Alexander had decided to break his fast, the serene surroundings having a calming effect on his overactive nerves. He studied his brother over the rim of the paper he was reading.

"Ye seem verra cheerful for someone who has lost the family fortune."

Christopher scowled but looked ashamed as he poured himself a cup of tea and added two cubes of sugar and a splash of milk. Stirring the concoction, he tapped the spoon on the side before dropping it to the table and addressing his brother. "I dinna need your constant reminder of what I've done."

"Nay? Ye think no'?" He folded the paper closed and tossed it onto the table. "I've been through the books. Did ye forget about everything I'd taught ye before I left? Ye're lucky I came home when I did. Otherwise, I would have come home to Millwool in someone else's hands and ye and the staff living on the streets."

"Ye over-exaggerate, brother." He sipped his tea with a roll of his eyes.

"I dinna." He studied Christopher. He looked better rested than he did last night. "Who has my sheep?"

Christopher blanched. Any color that he had drained away as he pushed out a breath, not meeting his eyes. "Ross."

"What?" He felt the urge to beat his brother, return. "Dougal Ross?"

"Aye."

Dougal Ross was one of the most feared debtors on this side of Edinburgh. There was no way in hell he would accept the same price for the sheep that Christopher had lost to him. Nay, Dougal knew how much those sheep were worth to Millwool, and he would expect to be compensated justly.

"Do ye ken what ye have done?"

"Och, aye. I do." Christopher said, glaring at Alexander. "I ken quite well. Ye willna let me forget, thank ye. If ye'd only let me—"

"Absolutely no'," Alexander cut him off before he could finish the sentence. "Ye've done more than enough damage." He pushed away from the table. "Looks like I'm going to have to pay a visit to Ross. Ye better hope he is willing to strike a deal."

"I am sorry, ye ken. I didna mean for any of this to happen."

Alexander held up a hand. "I dinna want to hear anything more. Ye can now run around without the worry of the household on your shoulders. But take heed, brother, stay out of the damn gambling houses. If I hear word of ye even stepping foot in one, I'll have ye locked in your room."

"Ye canna do that. I am a grown man."

Alexander spun and bent down so he was eye to eye with his brother. "Are ye now? Grown men ken their responsibilities. They dinna squander their livelihood on cards. 'Tis no' just ye that ye need to worry about. So many people depend on us. Are ye truly that selfish?" He gave Christopher a shove and left the room, paying no attention to the tea that sloshed from his cup onto the floor.

Dougal Ross was known to hang around the gambling houses, stepping in whenever someone lost big. Striking a deal that would leave the house paid and the gambler indebted to him. Meeting with Ross was going to be most unpleasant. He'd be lucky to leave there with a clue as to where his sheep were. Ross was good at making deals. But he was no farmer. He wouldn't have the slightest idea what to do with a flock of sheep. More than likely, they'd already been sold.

"Shite!" Alexander cursed as he walked away, fists clenched at his sides.

"HOW LONG WILL we be staying at Millwool?" Clarissa Gordon asked Gwen, her now sister-in-law. She tried to feign interest and appear nonchalant about their upcoming visit, but though she was sure she could hide her feelings from Nicholas, Gwen was much too observant.

"Your brother says at least two weeks. So, pack accordingly." Gwen picked up the blue gown Clarissa had removed from her wardrobe and laid it out on her bed. "This one is gorgeous."

It was one of her favorites. A beautiful periwinkle blue that paired well with her dark hair. She hadn't worn it yet and was saving it for a special occasion, whatever that may be.

"Is it too much? Should I leave that one?"

Gwen raised a brow in question. "Too much for what? Is there a particular someone ye may be trying to impress while at Millwool? Someone who happens to be the said Duke of Argyll?"

Clarissa straightened. "Dinna speak of such things. My brother will have your tongue," she snapped.

"I've no worry of your brother." Gwen laughed. "I've found he is much like a sweet puppy under that tough exterior."

"I dinna believe he would be happy to hear ye describing him as such," Clarissa quipped.

Gwen swatted the statement away and refocused her attention on the gown. "I think 'tis perfect. Most certainly we will attend a ball or two whilst we are visiting.

"Ye think so?" The thought of attending any event with Alexander Campbell made Clarissa's heart jump in her chest and had her pulse accelerating.

Her mind kept jumping to when Alexander had arrived at Huntly for Nicholas's party several months ago. When their eyes had locked, heat had surged through her body. It wasn't the first time she'd seen her brother's best friend. Quite the opposite. He'd visited often in their younger years. But it had been some time since they'd seen each other.

Time away in which they'd both grown. He'd always been handsome. Tall and broad, with thick, wavy black hair. The curls made it unruly and often, she wanted to tuck a wayward curl behind his ear. She would admit to sneaking many a glance at her brother's best friend as she watched the pair run around the grounds from afar.

But when she'd seen him after his return, those feelings flooded her tenfold. She was no longer a young lass. She was of marrying age. And her body flared to life with such a force it scared her. So much so that she had grabbed Gwen's hand and yanked her in the opposite direction.

"Have ye decided?"

Gwen's voice broke into Clarissa's thoughts, and she shook her head to clear her memories.

Gwen and her brother, Nicholas, had been married for a few months now. Gwen was her brother's match and equal in every way and she'd never seen him happier than when he met Gwen. And she'd fallen into the sister role naturally and happily. Clarissa surmised it was likely due to Gwen only having brothers. It was nice to have someone near her in age to talk to.

To discuss things with. Things such as men and marriage. It

was also nice to have someone to share the care of her younger siblings with. While her brother was away, their mother seemed to forget she had children, and the care fell to Clarissa. She didn't mind overmuch. She loved her family dearly. But she would admit that she was looking forward to the respite and just enjoying herself while she was away. She would have no one to watch over other than herself.

Clarissa sighed. The gown was too beautiful to be left behind. "I must take it with us. Mayhap 'twill be of use."

Gwen clapped her hands in glee. "Excellent choice, Clarissa. Now, hurry, we mustn't keep Nicholas waiting."

They set to work packing the rest of Clarissa's items and then sent word to have the trunk loaded on the carriage. Clarissa's heart thumped a steady staccato as the time to leave neared.

Would Alexander take notice of her? Or would he still see her as Nicholas's younger sister? Only time would tell. And she vowed to make him see her as the woman she was. She was getting older and soon would be considered too old for the marriage mart. But she would not just settle for anyone. Nay, she wanted Alexander Campbell. He would be her husband.

He just didn't ken it yet.

"Ready?" Nicholas poked his head in the room, smiling wide when Gwen turned her attention to him, his eyes softening with affection. "We've a good stretch of road ahead of us afore we arrive at Millwool. Let us begin our journey." He held out his hand and Gwen hurried to him and scooped it up into hers.

As they made their way down the hall, Nicholas spoke again. "Who kens. Mayhap ye will find a worthy suitor for ye whilst there."

Clarissa rolled her lips inward to stop her from blurting out Alexander's name. She already kenned what Nicholas's answer would be. He had warned her numerous times to stay clear of his best friend. The man was a true rake. But rakes could be reformed.

CHAPTER THREE

"**L**ORD ROSS WILL be with ye shortly, Your Grace. Please, follow me to the parlor."

Alexander dipped his head in thanks and followed Ross's butler down the wood paneled hall decorated with vines that were painted in blues and greens. Not the style he expected for Ross, but outside of word of mouth, Alexander didn't know much about the man who held his sheep.

He hadn't seen his flock when he arrived, but that didn't surprise him. The man did not have the pasture available to him on this estate needed for such an undertaking.

In the parlor, Christopher slumped into a chair. Alexander kicked his foot. "Sit proper. Have some dignity, brother. Ye needna show everyone your defeat." Christopher shot him a glare but straightened.

Alexander clasped his hands behind his back and paced the length of the room. Did he believe he would be leaving here with his flock today? Absolutely not, but he hoped to at least be closer to reacquiring them.

"Your Grace," Ross said from the doorway and Alexander turned and shook the hand Ross held out to him. "I apologize for your wait. Your visit was," he paused, glancing at Christopher, "anticipated. I, however, wasna prepared."

"Understood. As ye can assume, time is of the essence to ensure the well-being of my prized sheep."

Ross raised a brow as he studied Alexander and nodded.

"Please, have a seat." He stretched out his arm towards the empty chair across from his desk next to Christopher.

Alexander lacked the patience for small talk. "As ye ken, my brother fell into some difficulties at the tables whilst I was away."

"Aye." Ross's eyes shot over to Christopher, but his brother paid him no attention as he stared out the window.

Alexander had to tread lightly. The best approach would be to appear thankful for the help Ross offered Christopher in his time of need. As much as it pained him to do so, he swallowed his pride and continued.

"My brother and I canna thank ye enough for extending your services to him when his luck was down. 'Twas verra kind of ye, but as ye can imagine, the Campbell flock is the means to our livelihood. We will need them back. I'm willing to pay ye for the kindness ye extended to my brother and pay ye extra for your trouble."

Ross clucked his tongue as his eyes darted from Alexander to Christopher and back again. "Whisky, Your Grace?" He pushed away from the desk and went to the sidebar.

"Nay, thank ye."

The man just shrugged and poured himself a glass, before turning back to Alexander, swirling the amber liquid in the glass before taking a sip. He approached the front of the desk and leaned on it, pointing his glass in Christopher's direction.

"No disrespect, but your brother appears to have a problem."

Alexander slid his gaze to Christopher, who glared at Ross. Ignoring him, he focused his attention back to Ross. "I agree. 'Tis something I will deal with, but 'tis no' of your concern. We've other pressing matters at hand which is why we are here."

"Aye, your sheep. Noisy beasts they are."

A sinking feeling hit his stomach. "Ye havena harmed them, have ye?" Worry washed over him.

Ross barked out a laugh. "Nay, Your Grace," he paused for a sip of whisky before continuing. "But, alas, I couldna care for them either. I am no' a shepherd."

"Where are my sheep?" Alexander asked slowly for fear of jumping up from the chair and beating the answer out of the lender. Instead, he took a deep breath, forcing himself to unclench his fists.

"Last I heard your sheep were well. But I dinna have them."

"What do you mean?"

"Ye've seen my lands. I canna care for such a flock. Naturally, I sold them."

"To whom?" Alexander gritted out.

"An American."

"What?"

"Well, he is from America, but he has inherited Baron Kitt's estate. Something about being the only living relative left. He is quite brash and of course, uncouth, but trying to make his way into society."

"And he thinks taking possession of Campbell sheep is the best way to do that?" Alexander wasn't concerned with his temperament. Obviously, the man was daft if this was his way to cement his place in society.

Ross shrugged.

"Does he ken anything about raising sheep?"

"Of that, I've no' the faintest idea."

He stood and opened the appointment book on his desk, scanning as he flipped the pages. "My wife is hosting a ball tomorrow. Invitations were delivered last week. I assume ye have yours already?"

Alexander had no idea what invites they had received while he was away. But if Ross said they were delivered, then he would take him at his word. The man ran a business that Alexander would never involve himself in, but he had always spoken the truth whenever they had conversed.

"I assume 'tis waiting for me."

"Splendid, I shall see ye there. The American will be there as well. I will be more than happy to introduce the two of ye if ye havena connected afore then."

Alexander nodded. "Thank ye. I've friends arriving for a visit."

"They are welcome as well. Mrs. Ross loves an estate overrun with guests for a ball."

On the ride home, Alexander wondered if he would have time to get his guests settled and ready for the ball and manage a visit to the Kitt estate before then.

He didn't think so. He couldn't tamper his frustration as they climbed from the carriage and entered Millwool.

He could only hope the flock would be safe for one more day. He would have them home soon. His company would be arriving shortly, and as much as he worried for his sheep, he needed to be present for the arrival of Nicholas and his family. For the arrival of Clarissa. He couldn't deny that even though Nicholas was his best friend, he was most anxious to see his sister.

THE DAYS WERE getting shorter as autumn crept upon them, and the temperature grew cooler. Even so, the air inside of the carriage as they made their way to Castle Millwool was positively stuffy.

Clarissa was glad she had the foresight to bring her fan, which she whipped to and fro, trying to move the air about. Tired of the confinement, she sighed.

A sharp knock on the carriage wall made her jump and the coachman called out that they would soon be arriving at Millwool.

"Finally!" Clarissa huffed. "It feels like we have been riding for days."

Nicholas laughed. "Dear sister. There are much longer journeys out there. I dinna ken how ye would fare on such a jaunt."

Clarissa shifted in her seat. Her left cheek had fallen asleep from sitting so much and tingled with pins and needles as the blood started to flow again. "I believe I wouldna fare overly well, as ye can see, brother." She snapped her fan closed and stuffed it into her green reticule. It matched the gown she wore, a beautiful design the color of clover with an empire waist and a gold band of satin ribbon.

Gwen tried to hide her smile behind her gloved hand, but not before Clarissa noticed. "I, too, will be happy to see this journey come to an end. The fresh air will be most pleasant."

Castle Millwool came into view, its dark gray walls looked almost the color of moss in the light. It was a sight to see with its towers reaching high into the sky. The briny smell of nearby Loch Fyne seeped into the carriage and Clarissa took a deep breath, inhaling the salty scent.

As the carriage came to a halt, they waited for the coachman to open the door and set the stairs down for them to exit. She could see Alexander waiting in front of the steps that would lead them inside. He looked positively dashing in an Argyle tartan kilt and black waistcoat, his dark hair swept off his forehead, the curls tamed and gathered into a band of leather at the base of his neck. His strong, muscled legs on full display as he chose to wear black shoes instead of boots.

Her pulse quickened and her breath caught. She snapped her eyes away before Nicholas noticed, but Gwen had been watching her and gave her a sly smile.

Clarissa gave a quick shake of her head, silently pleading with her sister-in-law not to speak a word.

She breathed a sigh of relief when the door swung open, and Gwen stood without as much as a mutter. Thankfully, Nicholas was oblivious.

"Sister," Nicholas offered his hand to balance her as she exited the carriage.

Alexander stood so close now. She paused, biting her lip.

"What are ye waiting for? Ye couldna wait to arrive but thirty minutes ago," Nicholas said from behind her.

She snapped her head to him and rolled her eyes. But as she descended the steps, her foot caught on the last one and she stumbled forward, her arms pinwheeling out to catch herself from falling.

Alexander rushed forward, his strong arms enveloping her before she could hit the ground and steadied her on her feet. The heat of his hands searing into her arms.

"Well, that was not the welcome I expected, but I am happy to see ye, too, Rissa." Alexander chuckled, calling her by the nickname he gave her years ago. Still holding her, he swept his finger across her cheek, swiping a dollop of mud that had kicked up in her clumsiness.

Embarrassed, she pushed away from him, nearly falling backwards before she caught herself. Drats, it was as if she were a newborn fawn finding its legs for the first time. She stepped aside, far from the reach of Alexander's warm hands and made way for Nicholas to exit. His touch left her skin scorched and she fought the impulse to bring her hand to her cheek.

"That was quite the entrance, Clarissa," Nicholas laughed before clasping his best friend's hand. "Thank ye for having us, Alexander. Your generosity is much too kind, as always."

She felt the flush of embarrassment color her face. Nicholas's jab only added to her mortification.

"Nonsense, if ye are coming to Argyll, of course ye are going to stay at Millwool. What kind of friend would I be if I made ye find other lodgings?"

His deep voice flowed over Clarissa like warm honey. Gwen looped her arm around Clarissa's and leaned in close to whisper in her ear. "Dinna fash. I dinna think the Duke of Argyll minded catching ye. He looks quite handsome, does he no'?"

"Shhh! Dinna speak of such nonsense."

Alexander cocked his head in her direction, his twinkling brown eyes narrowing before rubbing his hands together. "I am certain ye are ready to clean up from your journey and fill your bellies. I've had Cook prepare a dinner for when ye are ready. Please, come in."

Clarissa couldn't help but think once she climbed those steps and entered Castle Millwool she'd never be the same.

CHAPTER FOUR

ALEXANDER DIDN'T WANT to let Clarissa go. Not when she felt as if she belonged in his arms. He kenned she was embarrassed, but she needn't be. She could have shown up to Millwool in rags, covered in mud from head to toe, and she would still be the most beautiful woman he'd ever had the pleasure to lay his eyes upon.

The urge to show Nicholas and Gwen to their room first so that he could take his time walking Clarissa to hers was strong. But it would be most ungentlemanly of him, so he ignored his want and played the part of a proper host. Leading the trio up the stairs and down the hall to the room he'd chosen for Clarissa.

He pushed the door open and stepped aside, allowing her room to enter. The chamber was bright with large windows overlooking the loch. The walls were painted a light yellow with darker yellow accents. It was the cheeriest room in all of Millwool.

And he thought it fit Clarissa perfectly.

Approaching the windows, she sucked in a breath. "'Tis a beautiful view. Thank ye for your generosity, Your Grace." She turned and dipped into a curtsy.

"Think naught of it. A beautiful view and room deserve a beautiful occupant." Alexander clamped his mouth shut. He wanted to kick himself.

Before she could respond, Alexander gave her a slight bow and took a deep breath of his own, trying to steady his body's response to the lass.

Gwen eyed him, a knowing look causing her eyes to crinkle and her mouth to lift at the corners.

Nicholas thankfully didn't take notice. Alexander would have to keep his emotions out of his best friend's sight. Hard as that would be.

Clearing his throat, he stepped quickly to the door. "I shall leave ye to freshen up. If ye are in need of anything, please do no' hesitate to ask. I will have it sent straightaway." He turned to Nicholas and Gwen. "Now, let us get ye two to your room. 'Tis on this floor as well."

"I ken Nicholas has given his thanks to ye, but I wanted to express mine as well, Your Grace. 'Tis most kind of ye when ye dinna have to go through such measures."

He paused and twirled to the couple following him and smiled. "First, ye dinna have to call me Your Grace. Your husband and I are of the same title. Unless of course, ye would like me to address ye as Duchess Gordon throughout your stay here at Millwool."

Pink tinged Gwen's cheeks and he couldn't help but laugh. "'Tis no' an admonishment. Ye can call me whatever ye like, truly. But I feel that we are more familiar with each other. Ye married my best friend. So, please, call me Alexander."

She nodded.

They resumed their walk. "But I will still address ye as Duchess," he chuckled as he turned to catch her mouth rounded in surprise. "I jest. Whatever ye would like to be addressed as, I will do as ye wish. Here we are." He stopped and pushed open the door and waited for them to enter.

As Gwen passed him, she gave him a warm smile. "Gwen is fine."

He nodded. "As ye wish," he said, returning her smile. Nicholas was lucky to find someone as special as Gwen. She was the first lass to see his best friend for what he was—a caring, kind man that loved deeply and with all his heart.

She saw past his scars. Something that had bothered him for as long as Alexander had known him. But no more. Nicholas could now be seen more often than not without the masks he always used to wear. Masks that would cover the right side of his face and prevent anyone from seeing his marred skin.

Gwen made him confident in himself. If Alexander had any interest in finding a wife one day, he could only hope to find a love as deep as theirs. But that day, if it even existed, was far, far into the future.

His mind wandered to Clarissa. Could she be that love? Absolutely not. What was he thinking? Clarissa could have any man she wanted. She was one of the most sought-after lasses of marrying age. What would she want with him? His reputation with women was kenned far and wide. 'Twas no secret that he had had many lasses warming his bed, sometimes more than one.

But the thought of any lass other than Clarissa did not appeal to him in any way whatsoever. Not anymore. Not since he'd returned from the war and visited Huntly. That didn't mean he was ready for a commitment. Nay. But a challenge? Mayhap. Though he had no desire to hurt her in any way. It was best to keep his distance so as not to be tempted.

Besides, in the off chance that he was struck by lightning and forgot all his qualms against being tied down to a single woman, he had nothing to offer Clarissa other than an estate that he had no idea how he was going to keep up and running if he couldn't get his sheep back.

"Alexander?" Nicholas snapped his fingers in front of Alexander's face. "Are ye unwell?"

He shook his head, clearing the thoughts of Clarissa to the recesses of his mind. "I apologize, I let my mind take a stroll."

Gwen clasped her hands in front of her. "The room is lovely. Extravagant even."

He'd chosen one of the wood paneled rooms for their stay. It had a large four-poster bed centered along the far wall, covered in blue and green linens and piled high with fluffy pillows. It didn't have as many windows as the room he'd given to Clarissa, but this one suited Nicholas much better. It also overlooked the garden. One of Nicholas's favorite things.

"Ye both should have everything ye need. I'll take my leave."

He closed the door and made his way to his study. Well, that was his intention anyway. But, instead, he found himself paused outside of Clarissa's door. The door that stood between him and perfection.

Was she undressing? Bathing? Both scenarios conjured up the most wicked of images in his mind and he had to stifle the groan threatening to leave his lips.

He forced his feet to move. To put distance between himself and Clarissa.

This visit would be the death of him. He could sense it.

Had he made a mistake in agreeing to her accompanying Nicholas and Gwen?

DINNER HAD LONG ago been consumed and both Clarissa and Gwen had retired upstairs to their rooms leaving Alexander and Nicholas to their own devices as they made their way to the study.

At the sidebar, Alexander poured two glasses of brandy and handed one to Nicholas, who accepted with a thank you.

The fire roared and crackled as they settled into the two overstuffed chairs arranged in front of it, watching the flames lick their way up towards the chimney.

Alexander took a sip, savoring the flavor before placing his glass on the walnut table between them. "Ye and Gwen are the epitome of wedded bliss. I can see it every time ye lay your eyes upon her."

Nicholas smiled. "Can ye?"

"Aye. I am verra happy for ye, Nicholas. Ye more than anyone deserves such happiness."

"Thank ye. She does make me feel like a Don. I ne'er imagined my life as 'tis now."

Alexander gave him a smile and focused his attention on the flames once again.

"And ye? Ye are in need of a wife as well. Family line, obligations, and all that."

He sighed and shook his head. If he wasn't so averse to commitment, mayhap Clarissa could be that woman. But he couldn't say that to his best friend. He didn't even ken if she felt the same about him. He thought so. The looks she gave him told him many things without saying a word, but she had not voiced any such feelings.

That was probably a blessing in disguise seeing how he was almost in financial ruin. Nay, he would need to cement his estate's future before he could even think about a pairing with anyone, especially Clarissa.

"No lass has caught your eye? Ye canna go around bedding all ye want with no commitment."

"Och. I ken that. No' that 'tis your concern, but I've no' bedded a lass since we've returned."

Nicholas's eyebrows shot up in surprise. "Ye arena serious."

"Aye, I am."

"How come? 'Tis unlike ye."

Alexander shrugged. He wasn't ready to bring up the subject of Nicholas's sister with him. Wasn't sure if he ever would be. "I have other pressing matters that have been of concern."

Nicholas narrowed his eyes and Alexander kenned his best friend didn't believe him, but he didn't press him for information. Not about the lassies. "What matters? Ye have been distracted since we arrived."

Alexander choked on the brandy he'd just swallowed. A rack of coughs making his eyes water. If only Nicholas kenned the thoughts running through his mind. He would not be happy.

Clapping him on the back, Nicholas chuckled. "Hell, brother.

There is naught need to get so affected by a mere question." He leaned back in his chair and sipped from his glass, studying the liquid as he swirled it around, a smile tipping the corners of his mouth.

Alexander, finally able to catch his breath, sighed heavily. "Christopher has been," he paused, searching for the right word. "Challenging since I've arrived back home."

Nicholas nodded, more than likely thinking he understood, since he had six siblings of his own that he had to wrangle. But he was certain none of his friend's siblings had ever gambled their family's livelihood away.

"Do ye care to expound on that? I ken Christopher has always been a bit of a thorn in your side. Especially after what he did to your books while ye were serving."

Unable to stop the laugh that burst through his lips, Alexander pushed his hands through his hair, scraping his scalp in frustration. His situation wasn't funny. Not in the least. But at this point he could only laugh.

"Well, ye may have noticed when ye arrived that the Campbell sheep werena on the grounds."

Nicholas tilted his head in thought. "Now that ye mention it, I did no'."

"Correct. That is Christopher's doing."

"Nay," Nicholas sucked in a breath.

"Aye. He actually gambled away the family livelihood. Hell's teeth, no' even only the family's, but the castle's, the village's, all the people we are responsible for."

"Ye no longer have possession of your flock?"

"Nay. 'Tis unbelievable, really. As if him running our books into the ground wasna enough, he added this."

"Who the hell takes sheep in lieu of coin for a game?"

"Aye, I wondered the same thing. Ross was involved."

"Ross!" Nicholas spat out his name. "He kens naught about keeping sheep."

"Which is why he is no longer in possession of them. He's

sold them off." Alexander pushed out of his chair and approached the fire, grabbing the poker and stabbing the logs. Sparks shot up in every direction, but he ignored them, taking out his frustration on the defenseless wood.

"To whom?" Nicholas asked.

"That's another thing. We've a new resident in town. An American."

Nicholas frowned. "Really? I havena heard, but I only ken the happenings around Huntly for the most part."

Alexander nodded. "Aye, he's apparently the only living relative of old man Seamus Kitt," he sighed. "And now that he is here in Argyll, he's looking for a way in to society."

Nicholas barked out a laugh. "And this is his way of solidifying that? He must be daft."

"My thoughts as well. But right now, he holds the upper hand. I talked with Ross today. He and his wife are hosting a ball tomorrow night. We are all invited. Apparently, the American will be there as well. I'm hoping I can talk him into selling me the flock back."

"Do ye think he will?" Nicholas finished his brandy and Alexander lifted the bottle off the sideboard and refilled his glass.

"I dinna ken. But I need to try. And pray that he will be willing to barter."

"'Tis a shite situation." He looked around the study. "Where is Christopher? I dinna believe I've seen him since we arrived."

Alexander shrugged. "He was with me when I paid Ross a visit. He left soon after we got home. I havena heard him come back. All I ken, is he sure as hell better no' be in the game houses. I warned him to steer clear of them, but he's stubborn. And angry." He drained his glass and poured himself a refill, drinking deep, wishing he could drink his problems away.

"What does he have to be angry about? Other than his own stupidity?"

"He's put off that I left him in charge of the books instead of hiring someone to take over the estate's finances. I had gone through the books with him before I left. Thought he was more than capable." Oh, how wrong he'd been. He should have gotten the clue when Christopher would look at him with glazed eyes as they pored over them, Alexander explaining the different transactions that needed to be paid and when.

Their predicament was as much his fault as his brother's.

CHAPTER FIVE

C LARISSA WOKE THE next morning to a pounding on her door. She rubbed the sleep from her eyes as she sat up and pushed off the covers.

"Who is it?" She grumbled, stepping into her slippers and slipping on her robe, cinching it at the waist as she made her way to the door.

The pounding ceased for a brief moment and then started again.

What time was it? She could not have slept in to such an hour that demanded such a rude awakening.

"What is it?" She pulled the door open, and Gwen almost knocked on her.

Her sister-in-law pushed past her and entered her room as if she hadn't just woken her up from a deep sleep in the most maddening of ways.

"Good morn, Clarissa."

"Is it?" She shut the door and turned.

"Aye. We've a ball to attend. Tonight."

"Tonight?" Clarissa repeated, shocked.

Gwen bobbed her head up and down. "'Tis why ye need to wake. We've much to do to ensure we are ready."

Clarissa fell back onto her bed, exhausted from yesterday's journey and tossing and turning throughout the night while thoughts of Alexander intruded her mind.

"Dinna sulk. There will be plenty of time for sleeping when

ye are back home."

Clarissa sat up. "That is weeks from now."

"Who kens, maybe ye will find your future husband at this ball," Gwen said cheerily, mirth lighting her eyes.

"I dinna want to find a husband, nor am I in need of one."

Gwen giggled. "Your brother says differently."

"Ugh, sometimes Nicholas can be incorrigible. Now that he's found happiness in a wife, he wants to marry me off."

"That is no' true. He only wants what is best for ye."

Clarissa eyed Gwen. Her sister-in-law seemed aware of her feelings for Alexander, but she had not come out and told her that she hoped to marry him. Somehow, some way. She had dreamt about it for months. Never mind that Nicholas would be completely against such a union. He would take a lot of convincing.

But then there was Alexander. He could have any lass he wanted. He was a duke. A very handsome duke, and she was sure that at whatever ball it was they were invited to, that every mother with a daughter of marrying age in near proximity would be there fawning over him. Batting their eyelashes, fluttering their fans and overly displaying their chests to entice him.

Which they more than likely would. Alexander was a known rake. Who was she to think that she could catch his eye?

"Alexander will of course be there."

It was as if Gwen could read her thoughts.

"Will he now?"

Gwen nodded.

"That has naught to do with me."

Gwen joined her on the bed and clasped her hands. "I ken ye are attracted to Alexander. 'Tis been blatantly obvious since ye saw him at Huntly. How Nicholas hasna noticed, I've no clue."

"It doesna matter. Nicholas would ne'er allow such a union."

"Why no'? 'Tis an even match. If I can marry a duke," she lowered her voice. "Which I still canna believe most days. My point is, if I can marry a duke, surely, ye, the *sister* of a duke, is a proper station to marry the Duke of Argyll."

Clarissa shook her head. "Ye shan't say such things. My feelings are my own and they will stay that way. Please. Dinna say a word. Nicholas mustn't ken. Or Alexander for that matter," she pleaded. "Neither of them can know."

Gwen sighed. "I truly think if ye explained your feelings to your brother, he would understand." She squeezed her hands. "And let us be honest here, one would need to be blind no' to see the affection in your eyes whenever he is near."

"Mayhap so, but it does no' matter. Alexander has a type of woman he chases after. I am most certainly no' that type of woman."

Sweeping her hand in the air, dismissing Clarissa's statement, Gwen stood, her hands on her hips. "I think we need to make him realize that ye *are* that woman."

Shocked, Clarissa looked at Gwen. "I will do no such thing."

"Why? This is your chance."

"But Nicholas…"

"Let me deal with your brother. I've some experience in that. He just needs to see the reason in it and when he does, all will be well." Gwen clapped her hands together as if she'd just solved all the problems in the world.

If only it were that easy. But as Clarissa thought about her sister-in-law's words, mayhap having her on her side wasn't such a bad idea. Clearly, she couldn't convince Alexander to marry her if she avoided him at all costs.

Nay, she only needed to enlist the right people.

Pulling the doors of the wardrobe open, Gwen peered inside. "Where is that beautiful blue gown ye brought? Ah, here it is." She pulled it from the cupboard and laid it out over the back of the chair. "Alexander doesna have any ladies' maids helping him here, why would he, since 'tis just him and his brother," a peal of laughter escaped her lips. Her sister-in-law was positively giddy. "But he did say he hired some for the time we are to stay here to help us with whatever we need." She snapped her fingers.

"They'll be here soon."

Clarissa groaned. "I ken your intentions are well meaning, but what will Nicholas say when he uncovers your scheme? I dinna want to be the cause of any strife between the two of ye."

Gwen paused as she riffled through the drawer where Clarissa had stored her jewelry. "Heavens no? Dinna ye see? This is perfect. Ye will be the bonniest lass at the ball. Your dance card will be full, and no doubt, ye will have suitors calling upon ye in the following days."

"Right. Why would I want that? I dinna."

Gwen rolled her eyes. "Obviously. But ye ken who else's attention ye will catch?"

Clarissa shook her head and drew her knees up to her chest, wrapping her arms around them. "I am quite certain that Alexander sees me as naught more than Nicholas's little sister."

"Bollocks," Gwen spurted.

Clarissa snapped her eyes to Gwen, her mouth open in shock. "Gwen!"

She dismissed her with a wave of her hand. "Och, ye have heard worse, I imagine."

"Aye, but no' from a lady."

Gwen giggled. "Well, before I became Duchess of Huntly, which is still quite strange to say, by the way. As I was saying, before I married your brother, my living arrangements were," she paused, a faraway look darkening her eyes. "Let us just say they werena ideal. A curse was needed here and there."

"Nicholas would be appalled to hear ye speak in such a way."

"He has heard," she confided with a wicked smile. "He rather likes it, in certain situations, mind ye."

Clarissa felt her cheeks heat and she brought her hands up to cover her ears. "Stop. I dinna want to hear about ye and my brother's," she couldn't get herself to say the words. "Ye ken."

Gwen laughed but dropped the subject. "This will be fun. Ye will be the belle of the ball."

She doubted that very much, but let Gwen continue to ramble on. She seemed very invested in securing a husband for her.

Almost as much as her brother was. The difference being that Gwen wanted her to marry for love. Nicholas only wanted to ensure that the union was beneficial to her standing. Annoyance had her flopping back onto the bed in the most unladylike way.

Why couldn't she choose who she marries?

Why should Nicholas have the final say? It wasn't his life that was being planned. He got to choose his wife.

She saw it as only fair that she be allowed the same consideration.

But she didn't have much time to wallow about her situation. A soft knock on the door and two young maids entered the room.

"Good morn, Your Grace, my lady. I am Louise and this is Ellie." Simultaneously, they dipped into curtsies, and set about getting everything ready.

"A bath will be drawn for ye. Then we can style your hair." Louise's eyes fell on the blue gown and lit up with glee. "Is this the dress ye are going to wear?" She picked it up. "'Tis beautiful." She studied Clarissa, her gaze roaming from head to toe. "I can picture it now. Ye will have all the gentlemen of Argyll asking for your hand."

Ellie shushed her and pushed her towards the door. No doubt to order the bath.

"They arrived quickly." Gwen waggled her brows. "Seems to me that someone wants to ensure ye have the help needed as soon as possible."

"Ye are incorrigible. They are here to help ye just as much as me."

Gwen smiled. "True, but we both ken if it was just me, such a fuss wouldna be made."

"We honestly have no such inkling." Clarissa pushed off the bed and padded over to the middle window and pushed the drapes aside. Her breath caught. The view was even more beautiful than Alexander had alluded to. The small waves of the loch lapped gently at the shore. Gulls circled above the water, no doubt in search of fish.

She had the urge to leave the castle and make her way down to the sandy beach. To let her toes sink into the pebbly sand. To feel the water rush over her ankles. She sighed, leaning her forehead against the windowpane.

"'Tis gorgeous, is it no'?" Gwen asked from behind her.

Clarissa nodded. "Verra much so. A walk would be divine."

"Mayhap tomorrow. After we break our fast, we can go for a stroll." Gwen squeezed her shoulders in a small hug. "I shall return to my room and prepare for the ball myself. Call for me if ye need anything."

"I will," Clarissa promised, knowing full well that she would not. If anything, she was trying to find a way to get *out* of attending the ball. She turned back to the loch. Her mind wandered and she saw herself and Alexander floating along the water in a boat that held only two. As he rowed, the muscles of his powerful arms would ripple as he spoke of the faraway lands he'd visited.

She sighed, shaking the vision clear.

She needed to find a way to stop Alexander from occupying her thoughts day and night.

But with the way thoughts of him warmed her insides and stirred feelings unfamiliar to her, it was no easy task.

With everyone busy preparing for their evening out, Alexander didn't have time to seek out the American. He would just have to have Ross introduce him to the man. He'd spent the morning reviewing the books, and though he had set money aside, he needed to use that to pay for the needs of his people.

He had very little to bargain with, and without Ross telling him how much he'd sold the flock for to the American, Alexander was going into the party with none of the necessary information that would help him in regaining his sheep.

Straightening in his chair, he stretched, his back cracking and protesting from being hunched over his desk all morning.

He needed to freshen up. His stomach growled loudly, echoing in the empty study. And eat. He had not eaten since early yestereve, and he and Nicholas had drunk too much while Alexander divulged all his worries.

The brandy had made his tongue loose and he had almost mentioned his attraction to Clarissa. Thankfully, he still had his wits about him, and was able to keep his secret. That was the last thing he needed to tell his best friend after revealing that he was on the brink of losing the estate.

He pushed away from the desk and stood, rolling his shoulders to loosen the tense muscles before exiting the study.

As he passed the library, he noticed the door was open. Surely, it wasn't Christopher. His brother had no interest in reading anything, except cards of course. And he did that terribly.

Curious, he peeked inside, and his breath caught. Stretched out on the chaise, nose buried in a book was Clarissa. He was too far away to see which book she read, but she was completely engrossed. She didn't notice as he approached.

She was dressed in a beautiful blue gown; the color accentuated her pale skin and dark hair, which had been pulled into a soft bun, with curled tendrils framing her face.

Quietly, he made his way behind her and plucked the book from her hands.

"Hey!" She quickly sat up in protest and stilled when she saw him.

Was that a good response or bad? He was unsure.

The book in his hand forgotten, he couldn't take his eyes off her. And when she looked at him with those big, chocolate brown eyes, he nearly lost himself.

"I was reading that," she said quietly, her gaze never leaving his.

He broke eye contact and turned the book so he could read

the title, *Mesmerismus*. "Ah, one of my favorites."

"Ye've read Franz Anton Mesmer?" She sounded surprised.

"Aye. Do ye think me incapable of reading?"

"Of course no'," she retorted.

Her cheeks were tinged pink as a flush crept up her neck. A neck he wanted nothing more than to run his lips over. He cleared his throat and tried to ignore the rush of blood to his groin. "Ye may be pleased to ken that I enjoy reading verra much."

She arched a brown brow as she studied him. "Do ye?"

"Aye." Her lips formed into the slightest pout. He didn't think it was something she had done purposely, but he had a most difficult time drawing his eyes away.

"Did ye enjoy this one?" Clarissa straightened, dropping her slippered feet to the floor. Her slippers matched the violet blue tone of her dress.

It reminded him of the flowers that grew wild in the fields.

Feeling more forward than he should, he pointed to the cushion beside her. "May I?"

She sucked her lower lip into her mouth, and he nearly lost the thin semblance of control he was holding on to.

She nodded and moved over, though there was plenty of room for him to sit.

He knew he was walking a thin line. Aye, it was only family here, but they shouldn't be alone. But that still didn't stop him from dropping down beside her. Didn't stop him from leaning close to her, inhaling her sweet scent.

"Tell me your favorite part so far."

"Of?"

He lifted the book in his hand. "The book."

"Oh," she laughed nervously, her thin fingers playing at the silver bejeweled necklace she wore.

Mayhap she was fighting the same feelings he was. Rules be damned, he leaned close and noted she didn't move away from him. Instead, her breath hitched, and caught in her throat as her eyes widened expectantly.

"Ye are a beautiful sight to behold," he said softly.

She lowered her lashes and looked away. "'Tis verra kind of ye to say. Thank ye."

They were so close. With just the slightest shift, he could capture her lips in his. Taste her as he'd been dreaming of for months. Her tongue darted out and wetted her parted lips. It would be so easy.

His body roared to life. The voice inside his head yelling at him to take the opportunity afforded him.

But he couldn't. Not yet. Not until he could secure his holdings and could offer her more than what he currently had, not until he could somehow get her brother's blessing.

For now, he'd focus on the book. "'Tis true. I—"

"What are ye two doing hiding in the library?" Nicholas asked and Alexander snapped to standing, the book that he'd held falling to the floor. Nicholas shot him a questioning stare.

"We arena hiding. We were just discussing books."

"Yes," Clarissa added. "Alexander was just telling me about his favorite scene."

"Was he now?"

"Aye, or I was just getting ready to do so until ye interrupted us." Alexander tried to keep his voice even so as not to pique Nicholas's suspicions while he bent down and scooped the book from the floor.

Clarissa stood and smoothed her skirts. "I must finish preparing for tonight. I was just taking a wee respite to relax." She stood on her tiptoes and kissed Nicholas on the cheek.

Alexander fought the surge of jealousy that flooded him.

"Ye do ken how much I enjoy reading, Brother."

Nicholas raised a brow at his sister's deflection but didn't say anything further. Hell's bells. The lass had only been here a day and Alexander could barely contain his yearning for her. It would take all of his strength to keep his temper tamped down at the ball tonight when every available man would be vying for her arm.

"Clarissa?" Alexander called.

She paused, just inside the door, and turned, "Aye?"

"May ye please be so kind as to allow me to have the first dance?"

Her eyes darted to Nicholas's and then to his. After a moment's pause and just when he didn't think she would answer him, she did.

"I would verra much enjoy that."

And then she was gone, and Alexander was left alone with Nicholas and his scrutinizing gaze.

CHAPTER SIX

DOUGAL ROSS'S ESTATE was lit with so many lanterns that Clarissa could see the aura of their glow on the grounds long before she saw the estate itself. The night sky illuminated in a welcoming golden hue. The carriage they—her brother and Gwen, and she and Alexander—rode in slowed as it approached the line of coaches arriving for the ball.

She was unsure of what had been discussed between Alexander and Nicholas after she'd left the library. But her brother's mouth was set in a stern line whenever his gaze fell upon her and Alexander.

Alexander.

Had she almost kissed him?

Aye, she had. His lips were so close to hers in the moment before Nicholas had barged in without a care in the world.

She supposed she should be thankful he'd done so. But, oh how she longed to feel Alexander's kiss. To have his mouth capture hers in the most decadent of ways.

She sighed loudly, trying to clear her thoughts.

But it was impossible.

Her hands were clasped on her lap, and she couldn't help but wring them together. Her nerves were on edge, jumping with a fiery intensity. Mostly because Alexander sat so very close beside her on the seat. His thigh brushing against her leg heated the whole right side of her body making her very aware of his presence. Every bump in the road deepened the touch and she bit her lip to refrain a moan from escaping her mouth.

If Alexander noticed her reaction, he'd remained completely neutral. Showing an amount of restraint that Clarissa could only wish she possessed. His hands remained on his lap, and just when Clarissa was sure their closeness had no effect on him, and Nicholas turned his attention to the window, Alexander discreetly reached out his pinky finger, stroking her leg through the material of her gown.

Her breath hitched and her eyes snapped to her brother, who thankfully hadn't noticed the gesture. However, Gwen's eyes twinkled with delight.

Nicholas turned from the window and Alexander broke the contact. "We've only a few carriages in front of us and then we can enjoy some fresh air."

Alexander cleared his throat.

Mayhap he was just as bothered as she was.

"'Twill be nice to stretch our legs," Alexander said, his voice clipped.

Mayhap indeed, but she did not dare look in his direction for fear of drawing her brother's attention. Having Gwen see was bad enough. Clarissa wasn't worried that she would say anything to Nicholas. She knew her secret was safe with Gwen. For now.

But Clarissa also knew that her discretion wouldn't last forever. At some point she would tell Nicholas. She could only imagine how her brother would react.

The carriage stopped and the door swung open. "After ye," Alexander offered.

Clarissa hesitated for a moment, then plucked her reticule off the bench and made her way down the step and waited for the others to disembark.

Gwen followed, then Nicholas, and then finally Alexander. He looked amazing tonight. He'd added a few accessories since she'd seen him earlier in the library. A sporran, which she tried to keep her eyes away from that area completely. He had the Campbell tartan draped over his shoulder, the clan brooch holding it in place.

"Shall we?" Alexander asked, sweeping his arm towards the entrance.

"Aye," Nicholas answered, holding out his arm for Gwen to loop hers into.

Alexander did the same, waiting expectantly as Clarissa's eyes bounced from him to Nicholas. Should she accept his proffered arm? Would people get the wrong idea? Would they start a rumor? She had already agreed to give him the first dance.

What would they say if they saw her arriving on his arm?

"Sister," Nicholas called to her, holding out his other arm so he could escort the both of them inside.

Worrying her bottom lip, she stole a glance at Alexander and noticed the flash of hurt in his eyes before he quickly masked it.

"Go on, lass. Ye must no' keep your brother waiting."

Still, she paused.

"Dinna fash. I will be right behind ye."

Nodding, she gave him a small smile and joined her brother and Gwen.

ALEXANDER FOLLOWED THE trio into the estate and paused as they were announced. He would be remiss to say he didn't want to be the one to escort Clarissa into the ball.

He did.

He wanted everyone there to ken she was his.

And he was hers.

Hell's teeth. What was he thinking? That because they shared a moment in the library that they were destined to be together?

It was as if he had an angel and the devil on each of his shoulders. The angel prodding him to pursue Clarissa and the devil jabbing him with his pitchfork whilst telling him a relationship was the last thing he needed.

But damn. He wanted to spend a day in the library with Clarissa discussing her favorite books and the parts she liked about each one. That she was well-read only added kindling to his growing fire.

As they entered the ballroom he had to tamp down the animal inside him wanting to claim Clarissa as his and scare anyone away that had the nerve to approach her.

But thoughts of their library encounter made him wonder if she was warring with the same indecision that he was. He wondered if she felt the same spark? To him, it seemed so, or mayhap that was just him being wistful.

Granted, they were far from making anything official, but if Clarissa said the word, he would pledge himself to her in a heartbeat.

His vantage point following behind her gave him a fantastic view. The sway of her hips as she walked ahead of him had his body roaring to life. He quickly averted his eyes and tried to focus on anything but the vision in front of him.

As Clarissa was announced Alexander could see all the eligible men in attendance perk up. Of course, they would want to marry the sister of a duke. A most advantageous union it would be for anyone here.

Including him, but that wasn't why he longed for the lass.

Nay, awareness dawning on him. After months of thinking about her. About not being able to get her out of his mind. He realized his feelings were deep and genuine. He didn't care about whatever dowry she came with. Hell, he would reject the dowry if it meant he would be given the permission to marry her. Because if he were ever to propose to her, his affairs would be in order. He would offer her naught less.

The Gordons entered the ballroom and Alexander stepped forward. As his name was called, he noted the fair share of women that focused their attention on him. He and Clarissa had much in common this night—eligibility.

A few months ago, he would have jumped at the opportunity

to be surrounded by willing lasses vying for his attention. His hand. His title. Not for anything serious, but he had had his fair share of lasses.

But now? Nay. None of them held his interest. They all seemed dull, and dare he say, paled in comparison to the beautiful Clarissa.

He descended the stairs and was immediately bombarded with mothers introducing their daughters. There was Miss Leticia Peregrine. Miss Prudence Wentworth. Miss Annalise Covington.

On and on the introductions went. He smiled and acknowledged each, but his mind was elsewhere as they prattled on about their likes and talents.

His eyes searched for Clarissa in the crowd, and he frowned. The poor lass had her own horde of suitors that were queuing up to introduce themselves.

The orchestra started and his eyes clashed with Clarissa's.

She'd promised him the first dance. And he was hellbound to ensure she kept that promise.

"Excuse me, ladies. 'Tis verra nice to meet all of ye. But I apologize, I am pledged to someone else for this dance."

He extracted himself from the crowd of women amongst their groans of disappointment and made his way through the crowd until he could reach for Clarissa's hand and lead her onto the floor.

With a look of relief, she accepted his offered hand and dipped into a small curtsy, hurrying away from the men—men who did not deserve Clarissa, he noted—and clasped his hand, resting her other on his shoulder as they twirled around the floor.

Her cheeks were flushed, a beautiful tinge of pink that brightened her eyes and gave them more of a sparkle than they usually held.

"Have I told ye how beautiful ye look this eve?" He meant every word he said. Clarissa could stand beside everyone in attendance and none of them would be able to hold a candle to Clarissa's beauty. Her elegance.

"I believe ye may have mentioned something similar in the library earlier."

Her eyes twinkled with a wicked gleam.

"'Til your brother so rudely interrupted us."

She laughed. The sound melodic to his ears. Everyone on the dance floor. Everyone in the room. All melded into the walls as if they weren't there sharing the space with them. Only he and Clarissa existed in this space.

"Aye, his timing was impeccable this afternoon wasna it?"

She ducked under his arm and spun, tapping her toe on the floor twice and then they joined hands again, and he led her around the floor.

"If I didna ken any better, I would think he was trying to interrupt our kiss."

Her eyes rounded in surprise at his forward statement. She looked around at the crowd around them to see if anyone had heard his words.

"Ye must no' say such things," she whispered. "Especially where people can hear ye."

"Ye wanted it too, did ye no'?"

"We shouldna have—"

"Shouldna have what? We did naught wrong. Naught happened. But no' because I didna want it to." He let his words hang in the air. For their meaning to sink into Clarissa's thoughts. He didn't want to leave any doubt about his feelings for her.

"Alexander," she breathed. The music stopped and they broke apart, bowing and curtsying as proper.

Viscount Heathton cleared his throat behind Alexander and broke into their unfinished conversation.

"Your Grace. Miss Gordon has promised me the next dance," he said meekly.

Alexander had to stop himself from rolling his eyes. This sod had to be delusional if he thought he had any chance at Clarissa's hand.

Clarissa lifted her chin defiantly. "Aye, I did." She dipped down to Heathton and looked back at Alexander longingly as the viscount led her off to dance.

His hands balled into fists at his side. He was certain the scowl on his face showed the man how unhappy he was about the intrusion. But he wouldn't compromise Clarissa in any way. If she'd promised the dance to Heathton, then he'd make sure she kept that promise.

But he didn't have to like it.

And he didn't.

Not one bit.

A hand clapped him on the shoulder, startling him. "Who's got ye all riled up, brother? Ye look ready to tear someone's head off." Nicholas asked from beside him.

Alexander tried to relax. To brush off the possessive thoughts running through his mind.

Nicholas's eyes followed Alexander's gaze and then snapped back to his. "Did ye meet Heathton? He's shown an interest in Clarissa. He will probably call on her in the coming days."

"Och, hell no, he willna." The words were out of his mouth before he could stop them.

Nicholas narrowed his eyes and then his brows raised in question. "What am I witnessing? Why do ye care who Clarissa—" his words tapered off as dawning washed over him. "Ye and Clarissa?" He asked.

Alexander remained silent.

"Are ye and my sister…"

He didn't finish the question, but he didn't have to. "Of course no'." Alexander spat.

"I ken that look. Ye want to. Ye want Clarissa."

Alexander found Clarissa on the dance floor. Heathton was talking, and she was feigning interest in the conversation. He could tell she wasn't interested because every time they twirled, her and Alexander's eyes clashed, and her look was scorching. But when her gaze returned to Heathton, they dulled.

Yet, the man didn't seem to notice. Nor did he ever run out

of things to say. The sod hadn't stopped talking since they'd started the dance.

"Ye canna have Clarissa." Nicholas stated, his voice low in warning. "We have already had this discussion."

Alexander met his gaze. "I would ne'er do anything to hurt her."

Nicholas shook his head. "That is no' my concern. Though your past with the lasses leaves much to be desired," he quipped. "After our conversation last night, what can ye offer her? Ye yourself said ye were on the brink of financial ruin. Ye could lose your estate. Then what? Ye expect me to want my sister to be destitute?"

"Ye ken I would ne'er let that happen."

Nicholas sighed, pushed his hands through his hair in exasperation. "Alexander, I love ye like a brother. I ken ye better than anyone. I ken your past. Your fear of commitment. Settling down. My sister needs better than that. Nay, deserves better than that."

Alexander opened his mouth to dispute what Nicholas had just said. But he couldn't. His friend was right. He didn't have anything to offer Clarissa.

And she deserved the world.

"Your Grace," Dougal Ross called from a few paces away as he wound his way through the crowd.

Alexander blew out an exasperated breath. He didn't want to deal with Ross right now. Nay, instead he wanted to find the largest decanter of whisky within his reach and wallow in his misery. But now wasn't the time. Instead, he plastered a smile on his face and acknowledged Ross.

"Ross. Thank ye for the invite once again. Your wife is most gracious to allow no' only myself to attend, but my friends as well. May I introduce ye to Nicholas Gordon, Duke of Gordon?"

"Your Grace," Ross dipped into a bow. "'Tis a pleasure to make your acquaintance. I hope ye and your family are enjoying yourselves up to this point."

"Aye, thank ye. 'Twas verra kind for ye to include us."

"Think naught of it. My wife always says the more the merrier." He turned to Alexander. "Your Grace, may I have a private word with ye? I mean no disrespect to ye, Your Grace," he said, addressing Nicholas. "'Tis in regard to the matter we spoke of yesterday."

Alexander nodded. "My friend is aware of the situation, but I appreciate your discretion. Is there someplace the three of us can speak away from prying ears?"

"Aye. This way, if ye will."

Alexander and Nicholas followed Ross out of the ballroom and across the foyer. Down a long hallway they entered a room with double doors on the left. They entered what Alexander guessed was Ross's study.

Nicholas's countenance was stiff. Alexander was certain he was not happy nor done with the conversation they were having when Ross appeared.

Ross shut the doors behind them. "Please, sit." He pointed to the chairs. "Would ye like a drink? Cognac, wine, whisky?"

"Whisky." Both Alexander and Nicholas said in unison.

Ross nodded and poured out three glasses, before handing them each one and keeping the third for himself.

"Ye're certain I can speak freely?" He asked, eyeing Nicholas.

"Aye. He is aware of my situation." The words tasted sour in his mouth. Clarissa entered his mind. Surely, she was dancing with someone else. Another suitor no doubt. He knew he didn't have anything to offer her right now. That would change. He felt it was too early for his best friend to dismiss him so easily as a viable suitor for his sister. As if he would ever hurt her. Put her in harm's way.

He would never.

Ross cleared his throat, and Alexander focused his attention on the man.

"As I said yesterday, your sheep are with the American now in charge of the Kitt estate."

Alexander nodded.

"He arrived no' too long ago."

Alexander pushed to his feet, the whisky sloshing from his glass onto the carpeted floor.

Nicholas rushed up behind him and grasped his shoulder. "Sit down, brother. Ye canna go out there charging like a bull. Settle down and think."

"I dinna ken how eager he will be to strike a deal. He's mostly interested in becoming a member in high standing."

"Then surely he would want to make nice with the duke of whose sheep he currently finds himself in possession of," Alexander stated.

"One would think," Ross agreed. "But I am no' so certain." He paused and sipped his whisky. "I dinna ken what his status or occupation in America was, however, he does strike me as conniving."

Nicholas frowned. "How so?"

Ross shrugged. "He gives me the impression that he would go to great lengths to get what he wants. Laws and morals be damned."

Alexander drew in a deep breath through his nose and exhaled in a rush. He just wanted his sheep back. To ensure their safety.

"How about this?" Ross suggested. "We approach the man. I introduce the two of ye and then ye can go off and discuss your options in private. Strike a bargain so both of ye are happy with the outcome. Beyond anything else, Kitt wants status."

"Ye will need to tamp down your anger to talk with him," Nicholas warned. "If ye do that, ye should be able to strike a deal."

"I canna believe I need to barter for my own flock. Christopher crossed the line with this stunt."

Ross lifted his brows at the mention of Christopher. "Where is your brother, Your Grace? I havena seen him at the tables as of late."

"Your guess is as good as mine. He left yesterday and hasna been home since." In the back of his mind, worry over his brother ate at his defenses. But his brother was a grown man. He should have kenned better than to gamble away anything that would hurt them and their holdings. Alexander found it hard to have sympathy for him at the moment. Mayhap after he secured his flock he would feel differently. But as of now?

Not a chance.

He rubbed his hands together, stretching his neck as if he were getting ready for a round of boxing in the ring. "I'm going out there. I'm anxious to talk with the louse."

"Well, then, let us go. I shall introduce ye straightaway."

Alexander went to follow Ross out the door and back to the ball, but Nicholas held him back with a hand on his shoulder. "Your anger is coming off of ye in waves. Cool it down."

He shrugged Nicholas's hand off. His words to steer clear of Clarissa still stung.

"'Tis none of your concern. I'll handle the situation."

Leaving the room, the music of a waltz filtered down the hallway. And though he was on a mission, he couldn't help but wonder who Clarissa was dancing with now.

Who was waltzing her around the dance floor? Whose hand was at her waist?

The thought had him balling his fists and stomping down the corridor.

CHAPTER SEVEN

I N THE BALLROOM, Ross paused, scanning the guests mingling, looking for Kitt.

Alexander scanned the room as well, but for Clarissa. He found her on the dance floor, stiffly waltzing with someone Alexander didn't recognize. She looked uncomfortable.

Her dance partner was small of stature. Lean and on the short side.

Anger roiled in his gut. "Excuse me gentlemen. I will join ye momentarily. My apologies." As if of their own volition, his feet moved forward until he was at Clarissa's side.

"Pardon the intrusion, but I believe Miss Gordon had promised this dance to me."

Clarissa smiled in relief and accepted the hand he offered. "Your Grace," she acquiesced.

Flabbergasted, the man just stared, open-mouthed as Alexander led Clarissa away and left him standing alone. He snapped his mouth shut and threw a glare towards them as he stomped from the floor.

One hand on Clarissa's waist, he clasped her hand in his other and took the lead as they swept around the floor. "Ye looked like ye needed an escape," he said, close to her ear. The urge to dart out his tongue and suck her earlobe into his mouth strong.

"Was it that obvious?" She giggled, tilting her head towards the floor.

He nodded and spun her around. "'Twas."

"I wasna trying to be rude, but the man had two left feet. I think he stepped more on my toes than he did the floor."

Concern knitted his brows together. "Are ye hurt?" He pulled away a bit, his eyes falling to her slippered feet.

"I'm fine. Ye saved me just in time. And my feet," she added with a laugh.

"Well, I am glad I could be of service." He pulled her closer, ignoring the people that watched them. "How many people have ye danced with tonight?"

Clarissa worried her bottom lip with her teeth, making it plump and dark pink.

The gesture shot straight to his groin, and he took a slight step back. This woman was going to be the death of him.

"Too many to count, I'm afraid."

"Any takers for the future Mr. Gordon?" he teased.

She chuckled. "Ye jest. I've naught interest in finding a husband here." Her eyes clashed with his at the word husband and they both sucked in a breath.

"None whatsoe'er?" he implored. Certain his feelings for her were reciprocated, he pushed. Knowing he shouldn't, but he couldn't help himself. No one here deserved to have Clarissa on their arm.

Barring him, of course.

Clarissa studied his face as they danced on but didn't answer his question. Did that mean she had found someone worthy of being her husband?

Was that person him?

Before he could ponder any further, the song ended, and they separated. He was about to ask her for the next dance, her dance card be damned, but Nicholas stepped in.

"I would verra much like to dance with my sister for this next dance if ye dinna mind?" Nicholas pierced him with a look that warned him to move on, and with a sigh, Alexander acquiesced.

He needed a drink anyway. And some fresh air. The punch in the gut feeling he got seeing Clarissa dancing with another man was unexpected. It would do him some good to get his emotions under control before meeting with Kitt. He was more likely to get what he wanted with a gentlemanly countenance rather than that of a mad dog.

"Well, look what the cat dragged in."

Alexander spun at the sound of the familiar voice. Finlay Primrose and Gunn Burnett stood there, arms crossed, smiles on their faces.

"I didna ken ye were attending," he confessed to his two close friends. He looked around. "Is Malcolm hiding around here somewhere as well?" He asked of their other friend. Including Nicholas, the five of them were a tight-knit group. As close as brothers. They'd grown up in the same circle. They'd gone to war together. Fought together.

Now that they've each returned to their respective homes, they seemed to only run into each other at balls and parties. Or weddings, like Nicholas and Gwen's. The group of them had been together to celebrate the special occasion.

"He is around somewhere," Gunn answered. He nodded in the direction of the dance floor, where Nicholas had just twirled Clarissa around. "Noticed ye getting handsy with Nicholas's little sister."

"Bollocks," he exclaimed, a little too quickly.

Finlay's brows shot up, a knowing smile on his lips. "No? Seems to me it was verra much aye."

"I was being the perfect gentleman."

"Didna say ye werena. Clarissa wasna complaining from what I could see, though Nicholas looked like his head was going to pop off his neck."

Alexander grimaced and looked over at Clarissa and her brother. He was probably telling her about how she should stay far away from him. Though she was a woman who thought she could make her own decisions, Nicholas was still the head of the family. What he said stuck. No matter how much Clarissa or Alexander wanted it to not be so. He only hoped Nicholas wasn't giving Clarissa too much grief. He didn't want to be the cause of such dismay.

"Are things all right with the two of ye?" Finlay asked.

Alexander blew out a breath. "Let's find a drink before we delve into such topics of conversation, shall we?"

"Och," Gunn elbowed Finlay in the ribs. "It must be serious."

"Ye are making much ado of naught, but I do need a drink." Even though he said the words, he wasn't sure he even believed them. He'd like to think things were fine between him and his best friend, but he also knew he was crossing a line. A line that Nicholas had firmly drawn in the sand.

And Alexander had ignored it.

"Your Grace, may I introduce my daughter, Evangeline."

Alexander sighed but plastered a smile on his face as he turned to meet the lass. The poor girl looked miserable and more than just a wee bit uncomfortable. She curtsied demurely and kept her eyes downcast.

Och, Alexander was sure she was a sweet lass, but he would go mad saddled to her. His wife needed to be spunky. Full of life. Not afraid to look him in the eye and tell him nay.

Like Clarissa. He sighed again. It was useless. Only Clarissa held his interest. His heart was hers. If she'd accept it. And if they could somehow convince Nicholas that the match made sense.

Damn, he needed to get to the American and regain his sheep. Then he'd have a chance at winning Clarissa's hand. Where had Ross disappeared to?

He gently excused himself from Evangeline and her mother and he, Gunn, and Finlay headed for one of the waiters carrying around trays and each grabbed a glass of whatever was being served, more than likely champagne. At this point Alexander didn't care. He just needed something to drown out his feelings.

In the most unrefined manner, he downed the glass in one long pull and placed it back on the tray and grabbed another.

The waiter gave him a look but said nothing.

"Whoa. There is certainly something amiss that we are unaware of. Tell us," Finlay ordered.

"Tell us what?" Malcolm appeared out of nowhere, drink in hand, clapping him on the back in greeting.

"What have I missed? Nice to see ye, Campbell."

"Ye have missed naught. Dinna let these two tell ye otherwise." He raised his glass in Finlay and Gunn's direction. "How have ye been?"

"Busy, but well. There are a lot of people that want things investigated."

"Really? Mayhap ye should put in for a position at Scotland Yard."

Malcolm barked out a laugh. "Nay thank ye. I much prefer working on my own terms." He took a swig of what looked like brandy and smiled at Alexander. "Enough about me. What about ye? I havena heard much from ye since returning from Nicholas and Gwen's wedding."

"Same as ye, busy." Alexander didn't expound on the details any further. He didn't need all of his friends to know he was a failure.

"Ye ne'er could lie," Gunn stated. "Your ears. They turn bright red. 'Tis a dead giveaway."

Alexander rolled his eyes. "Thank ye for noticing," he said sarcastically.

Gunn shrugged. "Are ye going to tell us what ails ye or no'?"

"Your Grace? Sorry to interrupt," Ross appeared from behind Alexander. "I, er, are ye ready for the introduction we spoke of earlier?"

That question piqued his friends' interest. They all looked at him, eyebrows raised, waiting for him to explain.

He didn't. He couldn't. It was too embarrassing.

"If ye'll excuse me, my brothers. I've some business to attend to."

Malcolm gave him a questioning look. "Need my assistance?"

Alexander shook his head. "Nay. Thank ye. I shall return shortly to continue with our catch up."

Following Ross, they passed the couples dancing, Clarissa and Nicholas amongst them. He couldn't resist the urge to catch Clarissa's attention. But her eyes met his right away. She gave him a small smile, and then frowned at whatever Nicholas whispered in her ear.

He sighed. He would prove to Nicholas that he could provide for his sister. Clarissa would want for naught if they were to wed.

"Ah, Baron Kitt. I'd like to introduce ye to the Duke of Argyll, Alexander Campbell."

Alexander assessed the man in front of him. The same man that he'd rescued Clarissa from earlier. *He* was the American?

"Your Grace," Kitt addressed him, giving him a low, flamboyant bow. He was dressed all in brown from head to toe. Suit jacket, trousers, boots. Everything. How dull. "I am happy to finally make your acquaintance."

Alexander gritted his teeth. The urge to throttle the man right then and there strongly pulled at him. Technically, the man had done naught wrong. He'd bought the sheep fair and square from Ross. His next moves would determine whether he was a man of upstanding ethics or a weasel, as Ross had suggested.

"I believe we have some matters of importance to discuss," Alexander paused and assessed the man. "If ye have the time, of course."

"TRULY, NICHOLAS, YE are being the most insufferable man on the planet right now." Clarissa complained. Every time her eyes happened upon Alexander, he would quickly spin her around so she couldn't see him anymore.

"There are plenty of other marriage prospects in attendance tonight, sister."

The song ended and she made her way over to Gwen, who held out a glass of champagne for her to quench her thirst.

"Thank ye, Gwen." She turned and addressed her brother. "I have told ye repeatedly, no' only tonight, but past nights as well, I am no' looking for just any husband."

"But ye need one."

She nearly stomped her foot as insistence. "I verra well dinna."

Gwen stepped up to Nicholas and placed her palm on his chest and Clarissa could see him visibly relax. "Dinna push her, dearest."

"We are running out of time before she is considered a spinster."

Clarissa choked on the sip of champagne she was in the process of swallowing. Whooping coughs escaping her lungs as she tried to catch her breath. She pointed a finger at her brother once she got the fit under control, ignoring those around her that were staring. "I will no' have ye calling me a spinster, brother. That is uncalled for."

Nicholas sighed and rolled his eyes. "I didna call ye a spinster, sister. I said that soon ye will be kenned as one. There is a difference."

"Why," she inhaled a deep breath to calm herself. Her voice came out much louder and more frustrated than she meant. "Then why do ye insist on saying such things, brother? Ye clearly ken I am no' interested in anyone here."

"Anyone?" He asked. "Sister, do ye mistake me for a blind man?" He lowered his voice. "I see the way ye are looking at Alexander. And I verra well see the way he looks at ye."

"'Tis naught."

"Bollocks."

Clarissa's eyes widened at his oath. People were starting to watch them. She did not need an audience to break down in front of. Grabbing Nicholas and Gwen's hands, she pulled them into an alcove where they could speak with some semblance of privacy.

"What is it ye have against Alexander, brother? He is your best friend. Is it because I am your sister?"

Nicholas looked up to the ceiling as if what she said was preposterous. "That is no' it at all."

Clarissa threw her hands up in frustration. "Then, please brother, enlighten me. Because I fear I am in the dark and I dinna want to be."

"Ye are making a spectacle, Clarissa," he warned, his voice low.

She looked around, and even though they've moved from the depth of the crowd, people were still shooting glances their way.

She lowered her voice. "If ye would explain yourself so it made sense, there would be no need."

"No need for theatrics. Really, there is no need for them anyway. I have told ye, there are plenty of eligible men here tonight that would be more than befitting of becoming your husband."

Clarissa's temper rose. Was smoke coming out of her ears, because she felt like there was? "And I have told ye, brother," she said. "I am in no need of a husband."

"Okay, ye two." Gwen stepped in between them. "'Tis clear that no common ground will be made about this situation here." She pierced Nicholas with a hard stare. "Mayhap we can agree to drop this subject for now and just commit to enjoying ourselves for the rest of the evening."

Nicholas clasped her hand and brought it to his lips. "Ye are always the voice of reason, love." He turned to Clarissa. "I will say this. Alexander is no' the man ye think he is. His past is colorful with many a lass that has tousled in his sheets."

Clarissa and Gwen both gasped at Nicholas's vulgar words.

Alexander's past was no mystery to her. She kenned well of his escapades. She didn't need her brother to remind her.

"I am well aware of that." She jutted out her chin defiantly, not caring that she more than likely looked like a petulant child.

"Well, are ye aware that he is on the brink of poverty?"

"What?" She asked incredulously.

"Aye. Did ye no' notice his flock of sheep were no' on his

lands?"

She hadn't really paid much attention to that. She kenned he owned sheep. Very expensive sheep that provided some of the best wool in all of Scotland. But she hadn't been looking for his sheep when she arrived.

"Exactly. Because he is no longer in possession of them. Without them, his estate is in dire financial straits."

Clarissa was aghast. She didn't ken what to say. Not because she cared about Alexander's money. She didn't. She was speechless because all she could think about was Alexander's future. What he would do.

Could she fix this somehow?

But Nicholas took her reaction the wrong way. "I told ye he was no' good for ye. Alexander is my best friend, but I forbid ye to pursue any type of relationship with him. He canna care for ye as ye need. I willna have this conversation again."

Nicholas stomped out of the alcove, leaving Clarissa and Gwen alone.

She swept at a tear that slipped down her cheek.

"Hey," Gwen cooed. "Ignore your brother. He means well, but sometimes he gets his thoughts discombobulated. He only wants what is best for ye."

"By making me marry someone I have naught interest in. That doesna sound like he wants what's best for me. Instead, it sounds more like whatever is best for him."

Gwen grabbed a napkin off a nearby table and dabbed at Clarissa's eyes. "Come on now. Dinna cry. We will find a way to fix this."

"How?"

Gwen tilted her head as she studied Clarissa. "Ye have true feelings for Alexander?"

Clarissa sniffled and wrung her hands together. "I dinna ken. Aye. No." She shrugged. "I am so confused when he's near. 'Tis as if he makes my mind forget how to operate."

Gwen gave her a knowing smile. "I ken exactly what ye

mean." She dabbed at Clarissa's tears. "Pay no heed to your brother. He will come around."

Clarissa took in a shuddering breath. "I am no' so certain."

"Give him time. 'Tis his job to see to your future and happiness. Once he realizes what will make ye happy, things will fall into place." She tossed the napkin onto a nearby table not being used and snatched two glasses from a waiter that was passing. "Here, drink up. 'Twill ease your nerves and make the rest of the night a little less stressful."

Quickly, too quickly, she emptied the glass.

"Better?" Gwen asked.

"Aye."

"Good. Now, let's get ye back out there." Gwen took her hand and led her out into the belly of the ballroom.

Within a moment's time, she was back out on the dance floor, this time for a jig, and though she had no interest in her dance partner, she couldn't help but have fun with the dance. She laughed and clapped her way through it, all the while hoping to catch sight of Alexander.

The song ended and she thanked her dance partner, who sadly, she'd already forgotten his name, and made her way to Gwen.

"That looked like fun."

"Aye." And that was all she said about the subject. She was too busy surveying the room to find Alexander. Had he left?

"I believe he's meeting with someone in one of the rooms." Gwen said beside her, watching the couples dancing, and not looking in her direction.

Clarissa relaxed, trying to act unphased, and more than likely failing.

"Did ye miss me?" Alexander said from behind her, and she spun around, unable to hide the wide smile that broke on her face.

"Where did ye go?" She bit her lip at her forward question. "My apologies. That is naught my business."

Unperturbed by her question, he brushed it off, but also didn't answer it. She followed his gaze as he surveyed the dance floor. The orchestra finished their short break and started playing again.

A possible suitor was approaching, and Clarissa stiffened. Sensing her unease, Alexander clasped her hand and headed towards the other couples beginning to dance.

"I believe ye saved this dance for me, Miss Gordon," he said loudly as they rushed past the man that looked suddenly dejected.

"Ye are bad," she whispered when they began their dance.

"Am I? I rather see it as gallant. Ye didna care to dance with him, did ye?" He tilted his head towards the man that was now standing at a table sipping champagne, daggers shooting out of his eyes.

"I didna, ye are right."

"Ye are most enchanting, Clarissa Gordon."

His confession took her by surprise. "I—"

"Ye need no' say anything. I find myself unable to control myself around ye. Words just burst through my lips at their own volition."

"Oh."

"I," he paused, as if searching for the right words to say. "I must confess. When I look at ye, I see things. I—" he stopped short before finishing the sentence, a faraway look clouding his eyes.

ALEXANDER NEEDED TO leave. Not the ball. But Clarissa's presence. He was ready to drop to her feet and promise her the world.

When he looked at her, he could see their future together. Their wedding. Their children.

Hell's teeth.

He dropped her hand and pushed his through his hair and blew out a breath. He needed to put space between them.

"I, um, I apologize." Thankfully, the song ended, and he broke away with a stiff bow. "Apologies, Clarissa. I must speak to someone."

He hurried away, leaving her on the dance floor, mouth agape. He felt like an arse for that. But if he continued to hold her, he feared he would never let her go.

Of all the balls Alexander had attended, he'd never had one turn to shite so quickly. When he thought about how the night would play out, it wasn't like this.

He blamed that bastard, Kitt. The introduction went fine, but the slimy excuse for a man said he had no interest in returning the sheep, nor selling them.

No matter the angle Alexander tried, Kitt shot it down. He was beyond frustrated and stalked away. He thought dancing with Clarissa would ease his mind. Unfortunately, it seemed to make things much too comfortable.

When visions of their future flashed before his eyes, he kenned he was in too deep and needed to extract himself from the situation. But the way he left Clarissa on the dance floor was uncalled for. No doubt it would draw unwanted attention to her. That wasn't his intention when he had pulled away from her.

Devil be damned, he had made a mess of things.

"What are ye doing?"

Nicholas.

"I've no time for your disdain right now, Nicholas."

"Pardon?"

Alexander snatched a glass off the tray of a passing waiter and downed it in one sip. "I am quite certain ye understand my meaning. I ken ye think I'm no' good enough for your sister. I've got it."

Nicholas frowned, then shoved him against the wall. "What the hell are ye going on about?"

"Ye've warned me to stay away from Clarissa. Ye've warned

Clarissa to stay away from me. Ye're pushing her to look at the prospects in attendance tonight when you damn well ken she isna interested and ye damn well ken that none of them deserve her."

"I didna realize your feelings for my sister ran so deep."

Alexander chuffed. "Did ye think I was just after a romp?"

Nicholas dipped his head. "Honestly? Your past with women doesna exactly give me the warmest feeling when it comes to my sister. I love ye, brother, but ye ken I must look out for my sister's best interests before anything."

"I meant what I said when I told ye I would ne'er hurt her."

Nicholas's eyes bore into his, as if he were searching. Looking for the truth to reveal itself in the reflection of his eyes. He nodded. "I believe ye. I do."

A wave of relief washed over Alexander. Like a huge weight had been lifted off his shoulders.

"But," Nicholas continued before Alexander could celebrate. "Ye still need to be able to care for her and provide for her needs. Your current situation doesna allow for such provisions."

"I understand. They will." He saw Kitt talking to Ross and dipped his head in the direction to show Nicholas where to look. "See the man talking to Ross?"

Nicholas's gaze tracked to Kitt. "Aye."

"That's Kitt. What do ye think?"

Nicholas frowned, his eyes narrowing. "Have ye talked to him?"

"Aye. He isna willing to negotiate."

Nicholas's gaze snapped back to Alexander. "He willna let ye buy your sheep back?"

Alexander shook his head. "Nay. It makes no sense. I think he wants something else, but I am no' sure. I am going to approach him again and see if I canna make any headway with him."

"Let me know if ye need any help. I hate to say someone oozes crookedness, but that man does no' look trustworthy in the least."

"I feel the same way. Wish me luck."

He stalked over to Kitt and Ross, his mind set on his mission. He'd been to war for Christ's sake. He could handle one American.

"Ross, Kitt," Alexander greeted the men. "I would like to speak to ye again, if ye dinna mind, Kitt."

The man sighed as if he were bored and then looked up at Alexander. Because he did have to look up. The man was nearly a foot shorter than Alexander. "I believe I have already told you I am not interested in whatever offer you have to offer."

Alexander gritted his teeth. Frustration mounting. "I will make it worth your while."

The man's brows shot up in interest. Ross cocked his head to the side, his eyes narrowed. "Will you?"

The bastard's eyes lazily swept the room until they landed on Clarissa, and he leered at her, licking his lips.

Fists clenched, he closed the space between them. Ross shook his head in warning to back off, and jaw clenched, Alexander kenned he was right. Willing himself to relax, he addressed the vile man that didn't deserve his time or money, and he sure as hell didn't deserve Clarissa.

"Let us retreat to the gardens so that we can speak with some semblance of privacy," Alexander suggested. He just really wanted to get Clarissa out of Kitt's line of sight.

They left the ballroom, walking under the ivy arch that had been crafted to lead the party-goers to the gardens.

It was much quieter out here. The light from the lanterns lit up the grounds and Alexander surveyed the area. Tall hedges trimmed in geometrical shapes adorned one corner of the garden. A huge water fountain sat in the center and was adorned with depictions of sea animals that swam in masonry and shot water out of their mouths.

The cool air was a welcome relief. With a majority of the guests inside and dancing, the room had grown quite warm.

Only a few couples wandered about, far out of earshot and more interested in themselves than anything Alexander and Kitt would be discussing.

"Well, you've got me out here," Kitt said, his American twang sounding foreign to Alexander's ears.

Alexander decided he didn't much care for the accent. Almost as much as he despised the man himself.

"You said you'd make it worth my while. Go on and get to it."

The man was positively uncouth. Alexander wanted to punch the smirk off his face. Instead, he drew in a deep breath and let it out slowly. "We've discussed my flock earlier. I do hope ye are caring for them as needed?" he implored.

"They're sheep. What is needed other than fields for them to roam about on? I've got plenty of pasture. They seem fine."

"Are they fenced in?"

Kitt shook his head. "No. There are no fences in place, but I don't think any have wandered off."

Alexander sent up a small prayer. "Have ye sheared them?"

Kitt barked out a laugh and slapped his knee. "You are a riot, Campbell. Do I look like a shepherd to you? I have no idea how to do such a thing. So no, they've not been sheared. They still have all their hair."

Alexander pinched the bridge of his nose, his eyes squeezed tight. The man was an imbecile. "I am willing to up my previous offer to buy my sheep back."

CHAPTER EIGHT

For the longest moment, Clarissa stood stock still on the dance floor, watching Alexander's retreating figure as he abandoned her.

She didn't ken what happened. They had seemed to be having a fun time. Even flirting if she dared to say.

Alexander's soft words so close to her ear had sent shivers down her spine. She felt an awakening in her core and found it so easy to lean into him.

But in a flash, something changed.

She was thankful he had waited until the orchestra had finished the song before he quickly excused himself and hurried away from her like she had the plague or some other vile disease.

People around her stared at his abrupt departure. She could see them whispering behind their hands. Surely, the move would be in the gossip papers in the morn.

No longer on the dance floor, she looked around the room. Saw the pointed glances. But even among them, she could not find Gwen. She saw Alexander talking to Nicholas. They looked deep in conversation.

No doubt her brother was once again warning him to stay away from her.

No reason for that. Alexander had made it clear to not only her, but everyone in the ballroom that he was most definitely *not* interested in her.

She walked the perimeter of the room. A waiter offered her a flute of champagne and she accepted it with a thank you. She sipped as she walked, looking for Gwen, but soon the stares were too much, and the walls of the room felt as if they were closing in all around her.

Fresh air. That was what she needed. After failing to find Gwen one last time, she gave up and made her way outside.

The cool air pimpled her skin and she fought off a shiver. She looked around and was grateful that she was blissfully alone. She rubbed her arms up and down to give them some warmth, careful not to spill her glass of champagne. Even the chilliness in the air wasn't enough to make her turn around and go back inside.

Nay, the fresh air would help clear her head. She descended the stairs and started a leisurely stroll through the rows of trimmed hedges. She could imagine the garden would be the epitome of beauty in the middle of summer with all the flowers in full bloom. The shapes were something she hadn't seen before.

It didn't compare to the beauty of Huntly's gardens, but she was sure her brother would love it nonetheless if he wandered out here. His love of flowers, especially rare blooms, was strong. He'd painstakingly tended the gardens at Huntly. As a matter of fact, that was how he'd met Gwen. She smiled at the memory of when Nicholas had finally caught Gwen as she snipped his orchids to sell on the streets.

Instead of being angry with her, he was intrigued. So much so that he would wait by the window, watching the garden to get a glimpse of her. She was the first woman that didn't look at the scars that marred the right side of Nicholas's face with disgust. She saw him for the handsome person he was, both inside and out.

Even if he was being obtuse when it came to Alexander.

Worried she had wandered too far away from the house, she turned to head back inside when she thought she'd heard her name.

She ducked behind a tall cone shaped hedge and waited. It

was Alexander's voice.

"What does Clarissa have to do with any of this?"

He was talking about her. To whom?

"She's quite," the other voice, sounding like it belonged to the American she had danced with earlier, paused. "How do you Scots call it, bonny."

Clarissa's breath hitched and her heart beat so loud she was certain they could hear it. Why were they talking about her?

"Ye leave Clarissa alone," Alexander's voice came across as a low growl.

"Here's the deal. You want your stupid sheep back."

She shouldn't be eavesdropping. She kenned it was wrong to do so. But she couldn't move her feet. It's like they planted themselves in the ground, trying to be a part of the garden themselves.

The American continued. "I want Clarissa. For one night."

"Aye, right," Alexander answered.

She sucked in a breath. *What?*

"You arrange for Clarissa to spend one night with me and you can have your flock back. No money needed. Come now. You'd be a fool to not accept such an offer."

She couldn't see them. Could only hear their voices, but Alexander had agreed. He didn't refuse the offer.

Was she being used as some kind of pawn in their business dealings? Tears slipped from her eyes, and she ran back in the direction she'd come from.

Fool repeatedly playing in her mind. She was a fool.

A fool to think that Alexander was interested in her.

A fool to think they had a future together.

A fool to think that she was anything more than a piece of property to be bartered over.

She burst into the house and crossed the dance floor, winding her way around the couples dancing until she got to the other side.

As if in a craze, she whipped her head around, searching for

Gwen and Nicholas. She wanted to leave.

Now.

She didn't care if they left Alexander here and made him find his own ride home.

She swiped at the tears running down her cheeks.

"Hey," Gwen grasped her shoulders and forced Clarissa to look at her, concern knitting her brows. "What is wrong? What has upset ye so?"

Clarissa shook her head. "I dinna want to talk about it. I just want to go home. I dinna want to be here anymore."

"All right." Gwen placed her arm around Clarissa's shoulders and led her towards the front entrance.

Nicholas looked at them questioningly, and Gwen just shrugged her shoulders.

Clarissa didn't want to tell them what she'd just overheard. It hurt too much. Nicholas had warned her, and she'd ignored him.

She knew of Alexander's past. Commitment wasn't in his vocabulary. Conquest was though, when it came to women.

Was that what she was? Another conquest for him?

God, she was such a fool. Now the tears that slipped from her eyes were angry tears.

She was mad at herself.

"Let me go find Alexander," Nicholas stated.

"No!" Clarissa cried. "Please, I just want to go home."

IT TOOK ALL of Alexander's famous control not to beat Kitt's face to a pulp. He was tempted. Oh, so tempted. The unbelievable nerve the louse had for stating such a proposition. No matter how badly he wanted to regain his sheep, he would never compromise Clarissa in such a way.

She's not property. And Alexander sure as shite would not use her as a pawn in whatever dastardly game Kitt was playing.

"I would suggest ye leave at once," Alexander growled, his blood boiling. "Because I canna promise that ye will be able to walk out on your own volition if ye dinna leave my sight right now."

Kitt must have sensed the promise of violence because he paled, leaving his skin ashen as if he'd seen a ghost.

If he hung around much longer, Alexander would send him to the afterlife.

Kitt spun around and hurriedly made his way inside.

Clarissa. Alexander needed to see her. But as soon as he stepped in the door his friends stopped him.

"Gads, brother. What did ye do to Clarissa?" Gunn asked, his beefy arms crossed in front of his chest as he glared at him.

"What?"

"Aye, she was crying as she left a few minutes ago," Finlay added.

"She left? She was crying?" Hell's hounds. Had he embarrassed her so much by abandoning her on the dance floor that she'd left crying? He pushed his hands through his hair, exasperated.

"I dinna mean to embarrass her. I kenned I shouldna left her so abruptly."

His friends stared at him, frowns on their faces.

"Well, I dinna ken what ye did, but it looks like ye've got some apologizing to do." Malcolm spoke this time. Always the level-headed one.

Alexander shook his head. This night really had turned to shite. "I'll call for my carriage."

His friends exchanged looks. "Aye," Gunn said. "They left in your carriage."

He threw up his hands. Of course, they did. How else would they get home?

"Are the three of ye going to stay at Millwool? Ye ken ye are welcome."

"We have rooms at one of the inns, but we can cancel. We

didna plan on staying long. Just thought we'd take a couple of days to catch up." Finlay looked around. "By the looks of things, we have a lot of that to do."

The ride to Millwool took too long. Thoughts of Clarissa upset repeated in his head and his heart hurt kenning he was the cause of her pain.

All because he was scared of what the future held. Clarissa was changing his beliefs that he'd long held onto. When it came to her, the thought of commitment, though it scared him, wasn't abhorrent and he was finding it harder and harder to imagine his life without her.

He only had to convince her that he was serious. That he would never embarrass her again. And he had to figure out the situation with his sheep. He needed to get his estate in order. It was as if the universe had looked at him and decided things were too easy and with a snap of its fingers, turned his life upside down.

Once the carriage stopped at Millwool, Alexander pushed the door open and jumped outside, rushing up the stairs.

Nicholas met him in the foyer, his arms crossed, mouth set in a firm line.

Shite.

"Where is she?" he demanded, knowing he was out of bounds for doing so.

"She and Gwen are in her room. Getting ready to retire for the night."

Alexander went to push past Nicholas, but he stopped him with a hand to his chest. "Dinna."

"I must apologize. I didna realize what I'd done would cause her such embarrassment. I must fix it."

Nicholas's eyes narrowed. "Ye are the reason she is upset?" he bellowed, his face turning red.

Alexander rubbed at his temples, his head starting to thrum.

"What the hell did ye do?"

"Christ, Nicholas. Ye act as if I sullied her reputation. I will admit, I may have left the dance floor with too much urgency, but the song had ended. I meant no harm or embarrassment."

Nicholas looked confused and sighed. "I dinna ken what is going on. She wouldna speak a word about it on the way home. She just demanded to go home and stayed silent the whole way. Then went straight to her room. Whatever it is, it can wait until the morn."

"But—"

"Nay," Nicholas cut him off. "Leave her be this night. She is verra upset. Gwen is with her. Mayhap she will clue her in as to what has happened."

The thought of Clarissa being upset all night didn't sit well with Alexander. He should be the one comforting her. Consoling her. It was his fault she was upset in the first place.

Finlay, Malcolm and Gunn joined them, and they stood around awkwardly for a few long moments, wondering what to do next.

"I dinna ken about the lot of ye, but I need a drink. Or two. Or a bottle," Alexander quipped, climbing the stairs and heading down the hall to his study. Ye all are welcome to join me."

"I canna say nay to a good whisky," Gunn stated from behind him.

CHAPTER NINE

Breakfast the next morn was a disaster. Not only were Nicholas and Gwen there, along with Alexander, but so were the rest of their friends.

Clarissa sipped at her tea and pushed around the egg and toast that was on her plate, a fine piece of china with a delicate rose pattern around the outer edge, she noted.

She had no appetite. She could feel Alexander's stare and refused to meet his eyes. She still couldn't believe he'd played her for such a fool. That she allowed him to.

Gwen had tried to pry the information from her last night, but she refused to say anything about it. To admit she played right into his hand was even more embarrassing than him abandoning her on the dance floor in front of everyone.

And she was the only one that knew about it.

"Nicholas," Gwen called, her voice laced with an edge of sweetness to it. "Clarissa and I were thinking about doing some shopping today. Mayhap a trip to the modiste."

Clarissa's eyes met Gwen's stare. They'd discussed no such thing.

Nicholas studied both of them before nodding his head. "A splendid idea, love. We will be here for some time. Ye will want to ensure ye both have enough gowns to get ye through the rest of our stay."

Clarissa rolled her eyes. She didn't want to go shopping. She didn't even want to be here at the table pretending to eat breakfast.

Instead, she would much rather be hiding in her room. Or, even better, in the library where she could lose herself in other people's problems and forget about her own.

If she could somehow manage it, she would be quite happy returning to Huntly this very minute.

She made the mistake of stealing a glance at Alexander.

He remained silent, watching her, his dark eyes hooded, his overall mood brooding.

She wanted to tell him that it served him right. But if she did that, then he would ken that she was eavesdropping on what was supposed to be a private conversation.

And she would then have to tell everyone else what was going on. She didn't need or want all of that out in the open.

Nay, she'd keep his conversation to herself. But that didn't mean she forgave him. Absolutely not.

She pushed away from the table. "If ye'll excuse me, I shall go get ready for our outing, Gwen."

The men hurriedly stood as a sign of respect, but she ignored them. She'd thought coming to Argyll would be a fun adventure. Different scenery from Huntly. No responsibilities or cares. A chance to explore.

A chance to see Alexander.

To see if he felt the same way she did.

But all she wanted now was to go home.

The halls were quiet as Clarissa made her way to her room. Millwool really was a beautiful castle. The wood-paneled walls of the corridor gave it a warm feeling. The high ceilings were lit with chandeliers holding dozens of candles. Above each chandelier, the plaster was molded into a wreath of flowers, allowing the light to play off the uneven surface.

The floors were dark wood that matched the walls, and a red carpet runner kept the noise of footsteps to a minimum. Which probably was why she didn't hear Alexander until he called to her from a short distance away.

"Clarissa," he called again. "Can we talk?"

"I really dinna have anything to say to ye, Alexander."

Confusion marred his handsome features. "Please, allow me to apologize."

She laughed, the sound echoing in the space.

He ignored her laugh and continued. "I shouldna have left so abruptly after the dance. I put ye in an awkward position and that was never my intent."

She tilted her head to the side as she listened to him. That. *That* was what he was apologizing for?

"I didna think about how that would look to others. 'Twas verra selfish of me."

She spun on him. "Is this really what ye are apologizing for?"

His brows furrowed. "Is that no' what ye are upset about? Rightfully so, might I add," he said quickly.

She threw her hands up in the air and started walking. "Ye are insufferable. Almost as bad as my brother."

"That is no' how ye were acting yesterday."

She stopped and turned back to him. He was close on her heels, and she did the only thing that came to mind. She put her hands on his broad chest and gave him a shove, knowing she was stepping out of line. "That was afore I found out I was just a pawn in some stupid game ye were playing."

"What are ye talking about?" he asked, eyes dark.

She laughed. "I heard ye. The conversation ye had in the gardens." She watched as what she said sunk in.

"I am sorry ye had to hear that. He had no right to propose such a thing. I can see why that would upset ye. But what I dinna understand is why ye are taking your anger out on me?"

She shook her head in disbelief. "Ye canna be serious. Why wouldna I be upset? To be used in that way. I'm supposed to be happy about that?"

Alexander pushed his hands through his dark hair, stress evident on his face.

"I think there has been a misunderstanding." He looked

around, for what, she didn't know. "Let's talk in my study."

"I've no interest in such a discussion. "It was quite clear that ye are willing to barter me to regain possession of your flock."

He smirked. Which only caused her temper to rise. She could feel her face heating up.

"I find naught comical about this."

"Well, ye would if ye actually *kenned* what was actually going on instead of jumping to conclusions."

This time it was her turn to be confused. "I *ken* just fine. I heard him make the offer. One night and ye will get your sheep back. No money needed."

"Aye, the louse did make that offer."

"See?"

"See what? I didna accept it. I told him to go to hell." Alexander looked flustered. "Jesus, Clarissa. What kind of man do ye think I am that I would agree to such a thing?"

Was it true? She hadn't stayed long enough to hear what Alexander had said afterward. He'd agreed after the proposal was put forth. There was no denying that.

"Ye agreed after he stated what he wanted. Ye said, 'aye, right'."

"Aye, I did." He tugged at the cravat around his neck, loosening the knot. "Because I couldna believe what I had heard. Once it sunk in, and I told him I would ne'er agree to such a disgusting deal, I came in to find ye and was told ye'd left upset."

Oh dear, had she really gotten everything so misconstrued?

"Wouldna ye be upset if ye'd just overheard such a proposal?

"Aye, but why were ye out there in the first place? Were ye alone?"

It was her turn to be flustered. "Dinna put this back on me. I did naught wrong. I was tired of everyone looking at me like I'd grown two heads after ye left like ye couldna get away from me fast enough. I needed some fresh air."

"I," Alexander paused. "I am sorry ye had to hear such a vile offer. I hope ye ken I would ne'er, I repeat, ne'er treat ye like property to be bartered."

He reached for her hand, and after a moment's pause, she slipped her hand in his.

Tugging her closer, she was flush to his chest, his warmth enveloping her. "Ye are much too precious to me. I would ne'er do anything to harm ye in any way. To dishonor ye."

With each declaration he dropped his head a little bit, until their mouths were just a breadth apart.

Her breath hitched. Was he going to kiss her? She wanted him to.

Eyes closed, she waited for what seemed like an eternity, before warm lips touched hers. The most erotic sensation swept over her, and she leaned into the kiss. His tongue sought entry into her mouth, and she parted her lips, allowing it.

She reached up, circling her arms around his neck, her fingers teasing the curls at his nape.

He pulled her closer and she arched her body into his. The feeling foreign but welcoming. She didn't want it to end. When their tongues entwined and danced wickedly together, a soft moan escaped from her lips.

She needed to take a breath, but she didn't want to break the contact. Didn't want the sensation to stop. Her belly was on fire. Her core heating. She wanted more. Even though it was wrong, she didn't care.

Pushing her against the wall, he leaned his body against hers, breaking the kiss, but trailing his lips down her neck. She gasped for air. Goose pimples broke out on her skin. It was so hot in the hallway.

And then she remembered where they were. In the hallway. For all to see. What if Nicholas came up? He would kill them both.

It took all her strength to push Alexander away. As soon as his lips left her skin. As soon as his body no longer covered hers, she was cold. She wanted the warmth he provided. Craved it. But it wasn't proper. They couldn't be found in such a compromising position. Especially after Nicholas had forbidden them from doing so.

"We must stop," she whispered. Her lips felt swollen from Alexander's kisses, and she touched her fingers to them.

Alexander looked like he'd been burned. His gaze snapped to the end of the corridor where the stairs were. "I find the need to apologize to ye again, lass." He gave her a wicked grin. "But I would be a liar if I said I dinna want to kiss ye again."

She blushed. Hard. She wanted to kiss him again, but she didn't say that.

"Ye should go back to your guests."

"Ye are my guest," he said quietly.

"Aye, but I had already left the group. What excuse did ye give for leaving? Dinna ye think my brother will get suspicious for ye being gone so long?"

Alexander sighed. "Ye make an excellent point." He grasped her hand and brought it to his mouth, his lips lingering on her soft skin. "But I would much rather stay here."

"Ye canna. Besides, apparently, Gwen made plans for me and her today that I must get ready for."

He nodded. "For that, I will let ye be to do whatever it is ye need to do."

She turned and started walking away, her legs so unsteady that she was certain she wasn't walking in a straight line.

"Clarissa," Alexander called from behind her.

She paused and looked over her shoulder at him.

"Dinna forget. I would ne'er agree to such an arrangement. E'en if I didna have feelings for ye, I still wouldna agree. Ye deserve the world, no' to be treated as property."

With that said, Alexander turned on his heel and headed back down the hall toward the stairs that would lead him to where everyone else was.

Finally in her room, she closed the door and collapsed onto the bed, sinking into the soft blankets. She couldn't stop touching her lips. Couldn't forget the feel of Alexander's lips on hers.

It was such a wicked sensation. She wanted to feel it again.

Alexander's confession of what really happened was like a weight being lifted from her shoulders. She'd thought everything he had done up to that point had been a game. A part of a bigger plan that he had schemed. She was happy to find out that wasn't the case, but also embarrassed with herself for believing that he would do such a thing.

She'd known Alexander all her life. She'd never known him to be anything but upstanding and loyal. A gentleman. After all, her brother would not be friends with any unsavory character.

A knock sounded and she called out.

Gwen peeked her head in. "Are ye all right? I saw Alexander come after ye." She shut the door behind her and joined Clarissa on the bed. Her eyes widened.

"What?"

A knowing smile curved her lips. "Ye kissed him!" She spurted out.

"Shh!" Clarissa shushed. "And I didna."

Gwen pointed at her. "Och, ye canna deny it. I ken that look," she giggled. "Dinna fash. I willna tell your brother."

She relaxed. "Nicholas would be most unhappy."

"Aye, but what he doesna ken willna hurt him." Gwen yanked on her hands and pulled her to a sitting position. "How was it?"

"What?"

"Dinna be so secretive. I want all the details."

Clarissa laughed. "I didna realize ye were so interested in gossip."

"Dinna be silly. 'Tis no' gossip when 'tis my sister-in-law. And since he kissed ye, I imagine whatever was upsetting ye last night and this morn has been cleared."

She nodded with a smile. "Aye. A silly misunderstanding. I thought Alexander had done something that was unbecoming and involved me. I mean, aye, the conversation I heard was about me, but Alexander defended me. I thought he hadn't."

Gwen looked confused but didn't ask for further clarification.

She stood up, sweeping around the room. "I dinna ken what it was, nor do I need to ken. But I have to say, knowing Alexander as I do. I canna imagine him not defending ye. I have a fun day planned for us. Let us get ready and leave these men to do whatever it is they do when they get together."

Clarissa smiled. No longer dreading having to go out.

AFTER BREAKFAST, AND once Clarissa and Gwen had left for town, the men decided to leave as well to a gentlemen's club.

Alexander was looking forward to the distraction after what had transpired in the hallway with Clarissa. He could still taste her on his lips. The act was selfish. But he found as she looked at him with her big brown eyes that he couldn't resist her.

The kiss was spur of the moment and shouldn't have happened. He'd completely gotten lost in the feeling of her body pressed up against his. The taste of her mouth, her skin.

He sighed. Clarissa had done the right thing by pushing him away, even if he didn't want to admit it.

At least one of them could keep a straight head in such a stolen moment. If she hadn't, he would have gladly continued on, trailing his kisses down her neck, her collarbone, lower to the swell of her breasts, then lower still.

Shite. He rubbed his face with his palms, trying to scrub her memory away. But nothing could clear the vision of her hooded eyes and swollen lips from his mind.

"What has ye so knotted up, Alexander?" Finlay asked. "'Tis as if ye are walking a tight-rope."

Alexander shook his head. "'Tis naught," he answered stiffly, not wanting to discuss Clarissa.

"Mayhap we can find ye a circus," Finlay added with a chuckle.

Nicholas sent a glare his way as they approached the building.

Pulling open the door of the club he let the others enter and then followed on their heels. The smell of cigar and tobacco smoke ebbed over him as he scanned the room looking for an open table that would keep them out of earshot of everyone else.

He walked through the crowd, dipping his head in greeting at a few men he recognized. Glasses clinked together and an echo of cheers went up from one group, celebrating an occasion.

Picking a table on the far side of the club, he pulled a heavy wooden chair from another table close by so they would each have a seat. As they waited for the barmaid to take their drink orders, they surveyed the room.

The crowd was light at this time of day, and the men that were here were all engrossed in their own conversations and celebrations to pay them any mind.

Most importantly, Alexander didn't see Kitt anywhere in sight. Which was lucky for Kitt. If the louse had dared show his head in here this morn, Alexander couldn't promise that he would be able to control his anger.

Not after what he'd put Clarissa through. He was still baffled that she would think he would actually whore her out that way. Of course, she didn't use those words, but that is exactly what Kitt meant when he made the proposition.

The bastard.

Drinks ordered, Alexander sat back in his chair and waited. Mayhap they should have gone to one of the boxing clubs instead. He could use an outlet to release the aggression that had been building up in him ever since he'd left Kitt in the gardens with a warning to stay far away from Clarissa.

The bastard just sneered. He had a set of bollocks on him, Alexander would give him that. For someone so small in stature, especially compared to Alexander's size, he didn't back down. His ego wouldn't let him.

But when it's only your ego that you have in your corner, it will falter sooner or later.

And Alexander planned to take him down. Soon. That's why he needed his friends' help. To come up with a plan.

"All right," Gunn said. "There is obviously something amiss. Now that we are here, with drinks," he picked up his glass in a cheer, then continued. "Tell us what is going on, Alexander. Ye usually arena so tight-lipped, or serious."

He smiled. His friends knew him too well. And if he was going to recruit their help, they needed to be aware of all the details. No matter how humiliating they may be.

With a deep breath, he started. "Nicholas kens some of this already, so it willna be a surprise to him, and ye ken some of the situation, but no' all of it." He took a sip of whisky and let the burn warm his chest before he aired out the mess he found himself in.

"My dear brother," he said sarcastically, "as ye ken, has a problem with the gambling hells."

His friends nodded in unison. They were well aware of his brother's addiction.

"When I got back home, the estate's books were in an awful state. Christopher had made some verra poor decisions and things werena looking great for us." He waved his hand in the air. "But ye ken that. What ye dinna ken is that when I next traveled to Huntly, for Nicholas's wedding, my brother decided to visit the gambling hells again—with the naïve thought that he would be able to win back any monies that had been previously lost."

"What a shite," Gunn murmured. "Let me guess, he only made matters worse?"

Alexander chortled. "Aye, ye could say that. A good card player he ne'er was, so his plan was doomed to fail from the start."

"He's still young," Finlay offered.

Alexander flicked his gaze to his friend. "But old enough to ken better." He finished his whisky and lifted his glass to gain the attention of the maid for a refill.

"I came home to find the Argyll sheep gone."

Malcolm's eyes rounded. "What do ye mean gone?"

"Just as I said. Gone. The whole fucking flock."

"Nay."

"Och, aye. He'd lost them in a final all or naught game of cards."

"I canna believe he did such a thing. 'Tis your livelihood." Finlay shook his head as he sipped his whisky.

"Aye. And now, that livelihood is at stake. Some shite American has my flock and willna let me purchase them back."

"Why no'?" Malcolm inquired.

Gunn's hands clenched into fists on the table. "Who is it? Why dinna we pay him a visit?"

Alexander laughed. "Och, I did that already. Dragged Christopher along with me. Well, no' to the American, but to Ross who originally took the sheep for payment, who then sold them to the American. Kitt is his name. He was at the ball last night."

"I dinna recall seeing an American there."

With a scowl, Alexander thought about how the man had danced with Clarissa and made her feel uncomfortable. "He was there. But stayed out of the way for most of the night." He kept the dance to himself.

Gunn leaned forward, resting his muscled forearms on the polished wood of the table. "So, he has your sheep. Will he no' let you buy them back?"

"At first, I thought it was monetary. I offered him higher than what I had been told he paid for them, and he wouldna e'en let me get the numbers out of my mouth.

"That doesna make sense," Finlay quipped.

Alexander wet his lips with his tongue. As much as he didn't want to say what had actually gone on with Kitt, in order for his friends to help him, they needed to hear the truth.

"I didna think so either. So, I approached him again later in the night. In an attempt to offer him more coin."

"No' to be intrusive, but do ye have the coin ye offered?" Finlay asked.

He shook his head. "Nay, but I was going to cross that hurdle when the time came. But it didna matter. Kitt is no' interested in money."

"What then?" Gunn asked.

"Status, for one. But what he really wanted was," he paused, eyeing Nicholas warily, kenning that he was going to be very upset at the next words to come out of his mouth. "Clarissa."

"What?" Nicholas pushed back from his chair and stood with such force the chair toppled over with a crash, drawing the attention of everyone in the club. He ignored them and glared at Alexander. "Explain," he gritted out.

Alexander looked around the room. People still stared, waiting to see what was going to happen next. "I will," he said curtly. "Control yourself, brother. We will need to keep our heads about us if we want to take care of Kitt."

Blowing out an exasperated breath, Nicholas righted the chair and dropped back into it. "Go on."

"He wanted to strike a deal with me. I could have my sheep back if I agreed to let him have Clarissa for one night."

Nicholas slammed his fist on the table, causing the glasses to clatter and once again, everyone to look at the group. The club owner glared at them, and Alexander shot him a look back, warning him not to intervene.

"I will fucking kill him," Nicholas spat. "With my bare fucking hands. I will throttle the life's breath out of the bastard."

"That is also the reason Clarissa was so upset last eve. She overheard Kitt's proposition."

"Where is he? I am going to make him sorry for ever leaving American soil."

Malcolm, being the voice of reason, spoke up. "Calm yourself, brother. We will make him pay for trying to strike such a deal, but we must be smart about it."

Nicholas's chest heaved, his fists clenching and unclenching, but finally, he nodded, grabbing his glass and draining it before slamming it onto the table.

Alexander was shocked the glass didn't shatter under the force.

"Let us assess what we ken and what we dinna." This is where Malcolm's skills in detective work would come in handy.

CHAPTER TEN

T HE DAY, THOUGH on the cooler side, was still beautiful. The leaves on the trees were just starting to change color, bringing a whole new vibrance to the town.

Clarissa and Gwen walked arm in arm down the sidewalk. They'd told their coachman to wait with the carriage and would call him if needed. They didn't need him following and watching their every move while they were away.

"Where would ye like to stop first?" Gwen asked.

Clarissa really didn't have a preference. There were so many places that caught her attention. A gem shop across the street would be fun to browse around in, not that she would purchase anything there. There was also a chocolatier that she would love to visit after they had tea. A bookshop. And of course, the modiste was a must visit since Gwen had mentioned that earlier.

"I dinna have a preference. I will leave it up to ye. But I am also perfectly happy strolling the streets and enjoying the fresh air."

Luckily, she didn't know anyone here, so she was free to walk without being stopped to chit chat or greet anyone other than the smile she gave to those she passed. She still couldn't clear what happened earlier with Alexander out of her mind. Were her feelings normal? She didn't ken. Romance was never a topic she spoke to her mother about.

Thoughts of her mother had her smiling. The lengths that woman went through to make sure Nicholas found a wife showed no limits. Thankfully, Nicholas had found Gwen because no matter how well intentioned their mother was, her choice of a match for Nicholas was horrible. He would have been miserable.

"How did ye feel when Nicholas first kissed ye?" The words were out of her mouth before she could stop them, and her cheeks flamed in embarrassment.

Gwen stifled a giggle behind her hand. "I remember it well. We were in the greenhouse." Her eyes took on a faraway look as she got lost in the memory.

A tall man passed them and dipped his hat in greeting as he walked past. Clarissa smiled back and waited for Gwen to expand on her answer.

When Clarissa had assumed she wouldn't say anything further, Gwen finally continued.

"No' only was it my first kiss with Nicholas, 'twas my first kiss ever. It was sweet. Gentle. Passionate. 'Tis hard to explain, I think. It sent this whirlwind of emotions through me and I dinna ken how to respond." Gwen turned to her. "Why do ye ask?"

Clarissa drew in a deep breath. "Since there is no hiding anything from ye, ye ken," she dropped her voice, "that we kissed."

"Och, aye. Dear Clarissa, it was obvious the second I walked into your room," Gwen said with a laugh.

"'Tis embarrassing to say. And wicked. Ye ken what would have happened if we were caught? But 'twas devilishly divine. My whole body tingled," she confessed.

"Ah, that's how ye ken it was a wonderful kiss," Gwen waggled her eyebrows in the most unladylike way.

They broke out into giggles and continued their stroll along the street.

"Oh, lemonade!" Clarissa noticed the vendor selling glasses nearby. "Let's sit and have a drink." She reached into her reticule for coin to pay and then, drinks in hand, they settled at one of the tables set up for patrons. It was the perfect spot to rest and talk. People bustling by or stopping for their own drinks, provided entertainment.

When she was younger, she loved going into town with her parents. She remembered how they would treat all of the siblings to the fizzy concoction. She cherished those memories. Before their father had gotten sick and passed. She missed him dearly, as did her brothers and sisters.

When he died, Nicholas was forced to take on the responsibility of the estate and the family. Something that fell on his shoulders at too young of an age. But he'd handled it well and took his duties seriously. Even when he was away, he'd ensured they had the support they needed. Financially, they were set while he served his country. Their mother was home to take care of the everyday tasks of the family. Unfortunately, she was much too focused on finding Nicholas a wife instead of her family duties.

As the eldest sibling after Nicholas, Clarissa stepped in to provide support to the younger siblings. They had always been a close family, but that just cemented their relationships.

"Mmm," Gwen mumbled, sipping from her glass, rolling her eyes. "I havena had a lemonade in years. Before my parents…" She let the words trail off.

Clarissa remained silent. She kenned it was a tender subject for Gwen, who had lost her parents in the most brutal of ways. She, like Nicholas, also had to care for her siblings, three brothers. But unlike Nicholas, she didn't have the means for such an undertaking. Clarissa was amazed at her tenacity. She'd fought and done everything she could and everything worked out in the end.

Clarissa was just happy that they had both found happiness in each other. They each had experienced their own personal hell. She could not think of two people that deserved it more.

"How about we visit the modiste after this?" Gwen suggested, changing the subject.

Neither of them really were in need of new gowns, but it would be nice to see what the local modiste created compared to the one back home.

Clarissa nodded. "Sounds like a splendid idea." They sat in silence for a few minutes. The soft breeze blew the loose tendrils of hair that had fallen from her barrette and fluttered them across her cheeks. She pushed at them and tucked them behind her ears.

Watching the people walk by—couples, friends, families—everyone rushing off to wherever they were going. Clarissa enjoyed watching them. The children most of all. More than one pointed to the lemonade vendor and plastered huge smiles on their chubby faces when they got their wish.

One day, she would love to have the same type of interaction with a family of her own. She had had lots of experience with bringing up her siblings, the youngest of which were a set of overactive twins. She had loved every minute of it, even if she was enjoying a little time away from them.

A butterfly flitted closely, its bright orange wings taking it from bloom to bloom of the flowers that were arranged in massive pots near the tables.

Sipping the last of her lemonade, Clarissa patted her stomach. "That hit the spot. What do ye think Nicholas and his friends are doing now?" she asked. Curious for any glimpse into what men did when they went into town.

"Och, I am certain they are at one of the gentlemen's clubs, talking about the devil kens what."

"More than likely, things we dinna want to ken about."

Gwen laughed. "Ye are probably right." She finished her lemonade and licked her lips. "Shall we carry on?"

"Aye. To the modiste." She held her arm out straight to point the way. "Are ye going to choose something?"

"Nay," Gwen shook her head. "I will just look to see what she has. Mayhap get some ideas to give to our own back home." She smiled wistfully, a faraway look in her eyes.

Clarissa studied her. Something was a wee bit off, but she could not put her finger on it and when the modiste's shop came into view, and they ascended the steps to enter, the thought left her mind.

Inside, the shop smelled of lavender and the space was warm and inviting. Bolts of fabric covered one full wall, stacked on racks for customers to see. Gowns, shawls, bonnets, aprons, everything you could think of were hanging on sale racks for those that didn't want their items custom made. On the far wall, a bank of mirrors was set up with a small dais in the middle. When someone stood in the center, they would be able to see themselves from all angles.

"Good afternoon, ladies," a middle-aged woman emerged from a cloth-covered doorway. "Welcome. How may I help ye?" She gave them a warm smile, her hands clasped in front of her. She studied Clarissa and clapped her hands. "I have just the gown for ye. Your coloring is perfect."

Clarissa and Gwen exchanged glances as the woman rushed about the shop, mumbling to herself about where she put the dress.

"Och! I believe I have it in the back. One moment, I shall go get it." She disappeared behind the cloth, and they listened at the sound of rustling fabric. "Got it!" The woman yelled to them. Bursting through the door, her arms full of silky scarlet material.

Unsure what to do, they waited and watched.

"Now, come here," the woman ordered gently, dipping her head to the corner of mirrors. "Ye must try this one on." She titled her head, assessing Clarissa.

The intense scrutiny caused her to blush, but she did as she was told and approached the woman.

"This may be a wee bit large for ye, but I can alter it without issue." The woman suddenly stopped. "How rude of me. I didna e'en introduce myself. My name is Alma, and I am the proprietor of this lovely establishment. I have the best gowns in town."

"'Tis verra nice to make your acquaintance, Alma. I am Clarissa and this is Gwen."

"I havena seen ye two around. Are ye visiting?"

"Aye. We're from Huntly. Visiting A—," she paused. She almost said Alexander, which would have been so wrong. "The

Duke of Argyll," she finished.

Alma's brows lifted. "And what did ye say your surnames were?"

"We didna. But we are Gordons. Gwen is the Duchess of Gordon."

Alma quickly dipped into a curtsy. "Your Grace. Forgive me for no' realizing sooner."

"Please," Gwen said softly. "No apology needed. We were just strolling through town to enjoy the day and noticed your shop."

"Well, I am verra honored for your visit." She looked at Clarissa as if she were waiting to hear a title that she had not mentioned.

"Miss Gordon is fine," she offered. Though Duchess of Argyll had a nice ring to it. She took a deep breath and blew it out. She did not need to have her mind running with such thoughts.

"All right then, Miss Gordon. I believe this gown will look positively ravishing on ye."

Ravishing. She would never describe herself in such a way.

"Step up, let's have ye try it on."

Clarissa glanced at Gwen, who just nodded and waved her hands at her in encouragement.

Alma pulled on a curtain that hung with wire and offered privacy while she helped Clarissa undress and put on the new gown.

"It compliments your color wonderfully." She pushed the curtain open and helped Clarissa step up on the dais.

From this angle she could see how the dress fit from all sides. It was loose around her waist and hips, not so much around her bosom.

Measuring tape caught between her lips, Alma moved around her, taking measurements, and grabbing pins from the pin cushion attached to her wrist and stuck them where they were needed to tighten up the fit. When she was done, she stepped back and Clarissa sucked in her breath.

The deep red color of the dress played off her thick black hair and the two melded together to make the perfect match.

"Ye look beautiful," Gwen whispered. "Ye must get this one, Clarissa. 'Tis fate."

Well, she didn't ken about fate, but she would be lying if she said it wasn't as if the gown had been made with her in mind.

What would Alexander think? She scoffed. Why was she thinking such thoughts? They would only hurt her in the end.

But it would make the perfect dress for Yule. If she could even hold off on wearing it for that long. Who kenned. Maybe a special occasion would arise that would warrant it.

She smiled at Alma. "I will take it."

"Do ye think it will really work?" Alexander asked warily.

His friends nodded.

"If the bastard doesna care about the sheep, then he'll be looking to offload them," Malcolm said. "And right now, it looks as if it may be your only choice."

Unfortunately, Alexander agreed. They had brainstormed different ideas all afternoon at the club until finally settling on hosting a livestock auction. Of course, they wouldn't host it themselves. They didn't have the means, and it would be way too obvious that they were trying to draw Kitt out.

Now, they were back at Millwool further discussing their plans.

"I will talk to Archibald Allen about the auction and what we are looking to do. I think he will be fine in calling it. Besides, he owes me a favor," Finlay said.

Alexander raised an eyebrow in question at his friend. "Why e'er would Allen owe ye a favor? Ye arena e'en here much."

Finlay dismissed him with a wave of his hand. "Actually, he owes my father. But doesna matter, I can collect in his name."

"What will your father say?"

Finlay shrugged. "Naught most likely. 'Tis been a while since he has been to Argyll. I dinna expect him to return any time soon. Dinna fash."

Alexander blew out a breath. "I pray ye are right."

But he worried that somehow, some way, something would go wrong. What if the auctioneer Finlay knew did not want to participate? What if Kitt refused to enter the flock up for sale? Surely, the man must be ready to rid himself of them. Alexander did not see him as the type to hold on to such creatures, especially since he hadn't the slightest idea of how to care for them.

He had his savings he had stored away. He could only hope that was enough to win the bid.

Finlay stood, ready to leave to meet with Allen.

Alexander followed him to the door. "I wish ye luck. Please give him my thanks."

Finlay nodded and then was gone.

He could hear Nicholas, Gunn, and Malcolm conversing in the study. He should rejoin them, but Clarissa had invaded his mind. He knew she and Gwen had returned before them. Their carriage was here and the coachman that drove them into town was carrying boxes inside.

He was surprised they hadn't crossed paths since apparently, they had arrived back at Millwool only minutes apart.

Torn between his friends and Clarissa, Clarissa won out, so he went on a search to find her. It didn't take long. She was exactly where he expected her to be.

The library.

He slipped in quietly, and for a few moments watched her as she read, her slippered foot tapping the floor.

Lightly, he rapped his knuckles on the frame of the door; he didn't want to startle her when she was so engrossed in her book. Yet she still jumped.

"Sorry, I was trying not to startle ye. But I failed."

Clarissa straightened in the high-back chair she was sitting in and folded the book on her lap, nervously tucking a loose strand of hair behind her ear. "Did ye need something?"

He almost groaned. Aye, did he, but he could never confess such things. "Nay. I noticed ye in here and thought I would see how your day in town went?" She didn't have to know that he had searched her out.

A huge smile brightened her face. "We had a lovely time. The weather was lovely as we strolled the streets. We visited the modiste and we e'en stopped for lemonade."

He smiled back, happy that she had enjoyed her time out.

"Ye can come in ye ken. I willna bite."

Again, he stifled a groan. Her comment was innocent enough, but thoughts of her teeth nibbling his skin had his body roaring to life and he folded his hands in front of him, trying to hide his body's reaction to her statement.

Stiffly, he walked over to the chair near hers, separated by a round mahogany table with a porcelain inset painted with flowers. "What are ye reading this time?"

She held up the book and he read the title. It wasn't a book he'd read before. It probably belonged to his mother. He certainly couldn't see his father reading such a tale.

"What is it about?" He wasn't overly interested in the subject, but he was interested in Clarissa and spending as much time as he could with her. If she wanted to talk to him about bonnets he would sit willingly and cling to every word.

The look she gave him made him think she was wondering if he was actually interested in talking about the book.

"I ask because I am no' familiar with it. It was more than likely my mother's."

Her brows creased. "I can put it back," she moved to stand, and he reached out, catching her hand.

Frozen in time, they both stilled. Her hand felt so small in his. The soft skin a direct contrast to his calloused hands. An odd thing for a duke, but he always preferred to do the work himself. Aye, he had staff that did a lot, but for certain things, his sheep, for instance, he preferred to be hands on.

He rubbed the pad of his thumb across her knuckles and caught the hitch in her breath. The pulse in her neck quickened and he fought the urge to nibble the delicate skin there.

"Please. 'Tis no' necessary. As long as ye are finding pleasure in it, then I want ye to continue to do so."

Pleasure.

A loaded word for his current state.

She pulled her hand away and he missed the contact immediately. Her eyes snapped to the door as if she expected Nicholas to come bursting through it at any moment.

"Are ye sure ye dinna mind?" She asked softly, her pink tongue darting out and wetting her lips.

The vision went straight to his groin.

He shook his head. "Enjoy it. When ye finish, ye will have to tell me all about it." He pushed up from the chair, not trusting himself to stay in the room much longer. The more time spent with her, the more he wanted to pull her into his arms and kiss the breath out of her.

Would she allow it? Mayhap. They seemed to both enjoy the other's company. But they had to get over the hurdle of Nicholas forbidding it.

He doubled back and leaned over her chair, his hands resting on the upholstered arms.

Her eyes rounded in surprise.

Not able to help himself, he lowered his mouth to hers, catching her lips in a soft kiss. He held himself back this time. Not like in the hallway previously, but he had the same response when he broke the kiss.

This lass would be the death of him.

She gasped when he straightened and he loved the way her fingertips went straight to her swollen lips.

"I would apologize for my actions, but I fear it would be insincere. So I shall no'."

He stopped at the door and looked over his shoulder. "In case

I didna say it afore. Feel free to use this library as if it were your own. 'Tis nice to see someone appreciate it. 'Tis been empty for far too long."

He didn't wait for her answer. He needed to escape her scent. It filled his nostrils and lingered on his clothing. On his skin. It was as if she enveloped him like mist. No matter where he went, she was there.

Instead of going back to his friends, he made his way up the stairs and knocked on Christopher's door. He had not seen him for a couple of days. Not since they'd visited Ross. And while usually his brother did quite well at staying out of Alexander's crosshairs, a couple of days was a new feat.

He waited a few moments more when no sound from within could be heard, and then knocked again, his knuckles rapping firm against the wood of the door.

Still no answer. "Christopher?" He called out but was only met with silence.

He pushed opened the door and stepped inside. The room was neat. The bed made. The drapes were open, and he could see the meadow where his sheep should be ambling about, grazing on the grass.

Stepping in further, he studied the room. It hadn't been used in a while. The water basin was dry. He walked over to the desk and noticed a folded piece of paper with his name on it.

Snatching it up, he flipped open the note and read.

Dear brother,

Please believe me when I say I am verra sorry for what I have done and the pain I have surely caused ye and the people that depend on us. I think it best, now that ye have returned, for me to take my leave and put an end to any more embarrassment of the Campbell name.

Your brother,
Christopher

Alexander blew out an exasperated breath and looked to the ceiling. He was afraid that Christopher would do something like this. He always preferred to run than face whatever consequences that came about due to his careless actions.

The only thing Alexander wished for was that his brother stayed safe. He knew that he couldn't lose any more of their holdings in the gambling hells. He'd already lost what he could, and now that Alexander was back and had removed Christopher's name from anything pertaining to Campbell holdings, there really was naught he could use.

Maybe he was off clearing his mind, cleaning himself up. Becoming a productive member of society.

Alexander had to laugh at that. One could dream, he thought as he pocketed the note, and left the room, closing the door quietly behind him.

"Is everything all right, Your Grace?" James said from the hallway. "I havena seen Mr. Christopher in a day or so."

"Aye. He has left. I dinna ken where, nor do I ken for how long, but I think 'tis safe to say 'twill be some time afore we see him again."

James bowed in acquiescence. "I will ensure his room is no' disturbed, Your Grace."

"Thank ye, James."

He headed back downstairs and entered the kitchen. Cook was standing over a steaming pot and turned when she heard him enter, her brows creased. "Are ye hungry, Your Grace?"

"Nay," he shook his head. He wasn't, but he wasn't satisfied either, if that made sense. He didn't feel satiated, but he was afraid no amount of food would satisfy his hunger. Nay, the only thing that could do that was currently occupying his library.

Cook cocked her head and studied him. "I'll make ye a cuppa then, Your Grace."

The cheery woman was always so good to him, he didn't have the heart to tell her nay, so he sat at the table in the corner and waited for her to heat the water.

"Has Miss Gordon asked for any refreshments?" he asked trying to make his voice sound casual. Uninterested.

Cook turned and smiled, her eyes twinkling.

She was too sharp. So aware, she picked up on everything.

"She hasna, but I heard her and the duchess had a wonderful time in town and enjoyed food and drink while they were out."

He nodded in agreement.

"She is quite bonny, Miss Gordon, isna she?"

Alexander perked up at the question. He knew it was a trap. She would not ask such a question if she didn't sense something there.

Unable to lie, he agreed. "Aye. Verra bonny indeed."

She moved about the kitchen, picking up the tin of tea leaves and setting the teacup and saucer on the table in front of him. "She had a couple of callers this afternoon."

"What?" He straightened, his back stiff. "Who?"

Who the hell had dared to come calling for Clarissa at his house? Somehow, this felt like a slap in the face to him.

"I dinna ken. James turned them straight away since all of ye had gone into town." She retrieved the kettle and poured the water into the cup, over the leaves. "I do believe they are going to return tomorrow.

Hell's teeth they willna.

Alexander would have to make sure he stayed home tomorrow. It would be rude of him to turn away a caller, especially since he had no right to Clarissa. She was not his betrothed. Nicholas had forbidden it.

He may not turn them away, but he would be sure to be present in the parlor when whoever called today came back.

Not that he was a betting man, that was his brother's area. But if he were he would bet his estate that one of the people panting on his doorstep tomorrow would be Kitt. That leech would have the nerve to show up and make an offer. Alexander almost laughed. Little did he ken that Clarissa had heard his offer.

No way would she accept him. Thankfully, Nicholas knew of

Kitt as well and would not allow him to get close to Clarissa, let alone agree to any type of union between them.

Speaking of unions, the thought of Clarissa marrying another man drove a spear through his heart. He wouldn't survive seeing her promised to another. Hopefully, Finlay was having luck with Allen. They would need to announce the auction as soon as possible and execute their plan quickly. The longer they delayed, the more he would lose Clarissa.

And his flock. But as the time passed, Clarissa was more forefront in his mind. He needed to ensure he could care for her.

And he would.

CHAPTER ELEVEN

THE NEXT DAY tensions were high as they all sat in the parlor. Clarissa plucked at an invisible piece of lint as Viscount Heathton rambled on about his hunting prowess. A fine quality to have, Clarissa agreed, but it was not a subject that she could spend the better part of an hour talking about. Nor did she want to.

As much as she wanted to, she couldn't tell him to go home because she had no interest in his hunts or him for that matter. Nicholas was huddled in a corner of the room, enjoying a cup of tea with Gwen. Every once in a while, he would lift his hands and push them in the air, trying to prompt her to engage.

But, Lord above, this man was a bore. She wanted naught to do with him.

Near the window, Alexander seethed as his eyes shot spears of fire into Heathton's back.

When James had announced Heathton's arrival, Clarissa was shocked. Was it normal protocol to call on someone that was just visiting? She didn't ken but found it odd.

Alexander had turned red as the gown she had purchased at the modiste the day before and his hands had fisted at his sides. But he had James show him to the parlor and refreshments brought in. Tea, sandwiches, and figs.

He had remained silent. Seething, but silent.

If he spoke, Clarissa was afraid of what might come out of his mouth.

"…and that was the second stag I shot on that particular outing. I have his antlers hanging on display in my study. The rack is quite impressive," his gaze dropped to her chest and her cheeks flamed.

Alexander's eyes bulged and Nicholas's head shot up to glare at the man, before one of them hurried over.

"I believe ye have out welcomed your stay, Heathton," Nicholas stated.

"But—"

Nicholas's eyes blazed black and Heathton snapped his mouth shut. He stood and gave her a quick bow. "Miss Gordon."

And then he was gone.

Clarissa breathed a sigh of relief. Finally, some silence.

"May I talk to ye about the partridge I shot when I was twelve?" Alexander jested.

"For the love of all things, that was the dullest hour of my life. And I have had some verra dull hours, but that, that was just horrid."

"I am sorry he took such liberties. He willna be allowed to call again. I will make sure of it." He smiled. "That is if he e'en wants to after Nicholas escorts him outside." He winked. "Either way, I shall inform James that he is no longer welcome."

She smiled her thanks and watched Gwen as she approached, a grin on her face. "Look at all the gentlemen tripping over themselves to assure ye are no' insulted."

Clarissa chortled. "I dinna think Nicholas counts. The man is my brother."

"Aye, but Alexander isna, and he was at your side quicker than your brother."

She sighed. He did come to her rescue in a breadth's time. Not that it mattered. Nicholas was still being obtuse when it came to Alexander. Just last eve, he had again warned her to stay away. For someone that claimed to be the man's best friend, he certainly did not think enough of him to make a good match for his sister.

The man was a duke. No higher station than the king. What else did Nicholas want? Shouldn't her happiness be taken into consideration?

Seeming to sense her plight, Gwen spoke up. "Give Nicholas some time. He will come around."

She slid her gaze over to her sister-in-law. "I am no' so certain of that. If he did, he would put an end to these callers. Can he no' see I have naught interest in any of them?"

Gwen bit her lip and nodded. "I think he is beginning to see. I catch him watching the two of ye sometimes. He only wants ye to have a stable home and be taken care of."

"And I only want to be happy," Clarissa spurted.

It was the same thing she had heard over and over again. *He only wants you to be taken care of.* She would rather be poor than tied to a horrible, boring rich man. Or worse, a man of means that treated her poorly. Why was it that Nicholas could no' see that?

"Viscount Heathton will no' be entering the halls of Millwool any longer," Nicholas said, entering the parlor. Standing beside Gwen's chair, he squeezed her shoulder and she leaned into the caress. "I am sorry for making ye sit through that, sister. The man was a cad."

"Ye can say that again," Alexander said from the door, where he leaned against the frame, his legs crossed at the ankles.

How long had he been there?

"I think ye should give Clarissa the afternoon off from callers, Nicholas. The poor lass just sat through an hour of the louse talking about hunting. As a man who enjoys hunting, e'en I found myself hating it the longer I had to listen to him ramble on. And then that last line? Completely unwarranted and vile." Alexander pushed away from the door and shook his head. "Heathton will be looking for a wife for a long time to come. Unless he comes across some desperate family that needs to marry their daughter off for whatever reason. And in that case, I feel sorry for the poor girl."

Clarissa giggled at Alexander's deduction. He was right. She already pitied the unknown girl.

"True. He didna seem so foul at the ball. But now we ken. If ye want a respite, Clarissa, by all means, take one," Nicholas offered.

But as she stood, James entered, clearing his throat.

"Your Grace, another caller has arrived for Miss Gordon."

Alexander sighed, his jaw clenching. It was nice to see that he was not enjoying this charade either.

"Who is it, James?" Nicholas asked.

"Baron Kitt, Your Grace."

Alexander pushed forward. "Och, hell nay," he spat. "I willna have him speaking to Clarissa. No'," he paused, pushing his hand through his dark hair, making the ends stand on edge and the curls to muss. "No' after what he did."

Nicholas pulled Alexander away to the other side of the room. Clarissa watched but could not hear what they were discussing in hushed whispers. Alexander fumed. His body tense and he looked like he was ready to burst.

After a few long moments, Alexander stormed out of the room, and Nicholas approached the sofa where she sat.

"I will leave this choice up to ye. Ye ken what he said at the ball."

She nodded.

"If we didna already have a plan in place, I would beat the bastard to a bloody pulp myself. But I canna. We need to be mindful of our approach."

Why was he even here? When they had danced, she most certainly did not give him the impression that she was interested in any way whatsoever. But she was thankful Nicholas was giving her the option to decline.

"I dinna wish to see him, brother. I would rather do anything but as a matter of fact."

Nicholas smiled and nodded. "I guessed as much. I will tell James."

As he left, he grabbed Gwen's hand and pulled her along with him. "I havena spent nearly enough time with ye as I have wanted on this trip." He nipped at her ear, and she swatted at him, her cheeks reddening, but she followed him out the door.

For a moment, Clarissa sat and enjoyed the silence, thankful she did not have to spend time with Kitt. She shuddered. The man made her nervous. The way his small eyes leered at her whenever she caught a glimpse of him.

She finished her tea and set the cup and saucer on the nearby table and stood to look out the window, which overlooked the garden. Not nearly as vast as her brother's garden at Huntly, but still impressive, nonetheless.

Waiting a few minutes to ensure that Kitt was no longer there, she watched the birds and butterflies flit about, enjoying the nectar from the late season flowers in bloom.

Once she felt she was safe, she left the parlor and was on her way outside when a warm hand circled her wrist and pulled her into an alcove.

She gasped, her heart nearly beating out of her chest as Alexander pulled her close. She clutched at her heart. "Ye nearly frightened me to death." She smacked his chest, the muscles hard underneath her palm.

He chuckled, low and rumbly. "I would ne'er do such a thing."

"Ye just did," she cried out.

"Shhh, ye dinna want to alert your brother to your shenanigans."

"Mine?" She lifted a brow at him. "I have done naught."

His hands dropped to her waist, and he pulled her even closer, so her body was flush against his.

"No' yet, but ye want to," he declared with a devilish grin.

She licked her lips. He was not wrong. She had been thinking about their stolen kisses and wanting them to happen again ever since. But she could not admit to such wanton needs. She rolled her lips inward, trying to think of what she should say to deter him.

"Come walk with me," he stated, his hands dropping from her waist, and he entwined his fingers in hers, pulling her out of the hidden alcove.

She tugged her hand, looking down the corridor.

"Dinna fash about your brother and Gwen. They are," he tilted his head. "How shall I say, otherwise occupied."

Her eyes widened when she figured out what he meant.

He laughed. "They are still newly married. 'Tis only natural."

"'Tis the middle of the day."

He waggled his eyebrows. "When temptation strikes, ye must take it." His eyes lowered to her lips.

Was he going to kiss her again? She had to fight the urge to close her eyes and lean into him, waiting for his mouth to claim hers.

"Let us go outside. The gardens are calling."

"Are they?"

"Well, mayhap no', but I saw ye admiring them earlier. I thought ye would like it."

She nodded and gave him a smile, allowing him to tug her down the hall. "I would verra much enjoy that."

Outside the sun was shining, but the air was crisp. Instinctively, she let go of Alexander's hand and wrapped her arms around herself. She should have grabbed her shawl from her room first before coming out.

Concern creased his brows. "Are ye chilled? Here," he tore off his waistcoat and wrapped it around her shoulders. "This should help."

"Thank ye." She grabbed the lapels and pulled them in close. The coat smelled like Alexander, and she couldn't help herself. She inhaled his scent, which reminded her of the woods with a touch of spice.

They made their way around the back of the castle to where the entrance to the garden stood. Two heavy wooden doors marked the entry. They were so tall, they even towered over

Alexander.

Pushing them open, he led her inside; he placed his hand lightly at her back.

"Which way do ye want to go first?"

Clarissa nibbled her lip as she studied the directions to decide which one she wanted to explore first. "Left," she said, choosing the path that had more fauna than hedge.

He smiled. "Excellent choice." He offered her his elbow and she slid her arm in his as they leisurely made their way deeper into the garden.

She commented on a few of the blooms familiar to her because Nicholas had them as a hearty mix to live through the cooler days of fall.

"Ye ken a lot about flowers," he quipped.

"Nicholas has always had a soft spot for his flowers. The more rare, the more interesting he found them. He spent so many hours in his greenhouse trying to get them to grow and bloom." The wind blew a tendril of hair into her face, and she swept it behind her ear.

"No' so much now that he and Gwen are married, but when I wanted to engage Nicholas in conversation that I kenned he would find interesting, I made sure I was prepared."

"How so?"

"Our library at Huntly is filled with books about fauna, flowers, plants, trees. Everything to do with gardening. Nicholas chose each one. I read them all multiple times, memorizing the types of flowers, what they needed to thrive, their native climates and environs."

"I bet Nicholas really enjoyed engaging in those conversations with ye."

She shrugged. "I believe so. I enjoyed them as well. The information was interesting even if I am no' interested in gardening myself. I just wanted Nicholas to ken I supported him. That I was there for him, no matter what he was going through." It also allowed her some time for adult conversation since so much of her time was spent with her younger siblings.

Alexander watched her as they continued to walk the pebbled pathway. "Ye are verra special, Clarissa Gordon."

IF ALEXANDER HAD thought he couldn't fall more in love with the beautiful soul Clarissa was, he was wrong. The things she did for her family—caring for her younger siblings while Nicholas was away and their mother was ill—along with what she had done for Nicholas.

He had never met a more genuine, caring person. She was selfless—almost to a fault. As they walked along the path, her slender arm hooked through his, he admired her altruism, but also thought she deserved to be selfish. Not all the time, but once in a while.

She had earned it for all her sacrifices. Sacrifices that everyone else benefitted from. Now whether they had acknowledged those things she had done for them, he didn't ken. He hoped they did. But he also kenned how most people were inherently selfish.

It took a special person to only think of others without a care for one's own self.

Clarissa was that special person.

He wanted to give her the world.

She stepped on a loose rock and lost her footing, grasping at his arm as she tried to prevent herself from tripping forward.

He wrapped his arms around her so she could catch her balance. Once he was sure she was steady, he let go, though he didn't want to.

"Apologies," she mumbled. "I am usually no' the clumsy sort," she confessed.

"I shall have that rock punished at once," he jested.

Blessing him with the brightest smile, her laughter hung in the air as she tucked her windswept hair behind her ear.

His body roared to life in reaction. Gads, he was torturing himself with how close he had been keeping her to him.

"I do no' think the rock will take heed, Your Grace," she said with a twinkle in her big, brown eyes.

Och, the way she addressed him by his title. Normally, he could care less. 'Twas way too proper for his liking, but when the words slipped from Clarissa's lips, they took on a whole new meaning.

"I am afraid I will have to take more stringent actions then. Its behavior must no' be tolerated." He loved their banter. The ease at which it came so naturally.

He didn't ken how he had thought he was happy when he used to go from one lass to another, not caring about their feelings, or that they wanted to see him again when he had no interest. He was a jerk. He would agree with Nicholas about that.

Clarissa had changed his outlook. She had him wishing that she was the one he was awakening all his desires with. He supposed she was, really. He had never had feelings for any of those other women. They were a release. A way to lose himself for a short time and then move on to the next. No emotions involved.

But with Clarissa, all he had was emotions.

"What is this that I have heard about a livestock auction?" Clarissa asked, breaking into his thoughts.

They came upon an elaborate water fountain in the middle of a small water source, filled with lily pads. It was one of his favorite spots to sit and think when he wanted to be alone. Now he wanted to share the space with Clarissa.

"Let's sit and rest our feet."

She quirked an eyebrow at him, but she nodded.

Settling on the bench, with their thighs touching, all sorts of thoughts ran through his mind. Rakish thoughts. He took a deep breath and let it out slow. His body wasn't cooperating either. If he had to stand right now, his body would betray him.

"Is it something I am no' supposed to ken about?" She asked.

"Pardon?"

"The livestock auction. I shall pretend I didna hear a thing if need be." She made a motion of locking her lips and then tossed the 'key' over her shoulder.

He chuckled. "Nay, no' at all. 'Tis public knowledge. 'Tis my turn to apologize. I must confess my mind wandered for a moment."

And wandered it had.

He rubbed his palms on his thighs. "I am hoping that the event will be a way for me to regain my flock and get them back on Campbell lands."

"Ye miss them."

It wasn't a question but rather a statement.

He nodded. "Aye. 'Tis silly I ken. They are but animals."

She turned to face him and shook her head, her brown eyes boring into his. "'Tis no'. No' at all. I find it," she tilted her head, searching for the right word, "endearing."

With a chortle, he broke their eye contact.

"I am serious. 'Tis quite evident ye care verra much for them. The worry ye have over them creases your forehead." She reached out, her fingers feathering over the skin of his brow.

His breath caught in his throat.

Palming his cheeks, she forced him to look at her. "I ken how much those sheep mean to ye. To your family. Your people."

He closed his eyes, captivated by her touch and her words. Turning his face, he kissed her palm, and when he opened his eyes, she was so close. Just a few inches more and he could capture her mouth in his.

A pair of crested tits landed on a nearby tree, chittering loudly and breaking the spell. He leaned out of her touch, and they watched as the two birds flitted about, chasing each other from one branch to another.

"I have full confidence in ye that ye will be able to regain ownership. Ye've worked too hard, and they are rightfully yours."

At a loss for words, he just nodded and continued to watch

the birds.

"It irks me that ye have to go to such great lengths for them when they already belong to ye. E'eryone kens they belong to ye as well. One would have to be daft to bid against ye at the auction."

He smiled. Her innocence in how the minds of men worked was sweet. Jacob Kitt was someone he'd only met recently, but it didn't take a genius to ken the lout was of unsavory character.

Alexander feared that the bastard would go to great lengths to prevent him from getting what he wanted. But he would do what was necessary. Somehow, some way, he would make things right.

"Ye are verra kind to say such things."

"I only speak the truth, Your Grace."

His heart tugged. The emotional turmoil this beautiful lass caused him was getting harder and harder to ignore.

Standing, he held out his hand to Clarissa. At the sudden movement, the pair of birds skittered away. "Shall we continue?"

Her small hand was warm in his and he gave it a gentle squeeze.

"I should return to the house. We dinna want to be out here too long afore people become suspicious."

"I can escort ye back."

She shook her head. "No need, though I thank ye for the offer." She looked around the garden. "And I thank ye for the tour. Your gardens are lovely." She dipped into a curtsy before turning and heading towards the castle.

He watched her walk away, his heart feeling as if it had been abandoned. His eyes caught movement in one of the upper windows. Looking down at him were Gwen and Nicholas. Nicholas had his arms crossed as he watched from above. Gwen was speaking to him, but he wasn't looking at her.

She swatted at his arm and pointed towards them.

Alexander had naught idea what they were discussing, but it clearly looked to be about him and Clarissa. He sighed. How could he get his best friend to see that he was falling in love with his sister? And that his feelings were true. Not something to pass in the night.

His mind made up, he, too, headed into the castle. He needed to talk to his best friend.

Inside, the corridors were quiet. He didn't ken where Clarissa had disappeared to. Probably to her room. Upstairs, he made his way to the drawing room, as he neared, he heard his name and he slowed to listen.

Feeling a wee bit guilty for eavesdropping, he was just about to make his presence known, but dismissed that idea as he also heard Clarissa's name.

"Ye saw the way Clarissa looked at him."

"Aye," Nicholas grunted.

"Do ye not realize that she is in love with him, and that he is in love with her?" Gwen said softly.

Love? Is that what he was feeling. Did he *love* Clarissa?

He did. Realization dawned on him as if he'd taken a rock to the head. He *loved* her.

Nicholas's sigh reached Alexander in the hall. He leaned forward, peering into the room. "Aye," he repeated. "But he is no position to provide for her."

"Dinna be ridiculous, Nicholas. People said negative things about us as well, but did that deter us?" She didn't wait for his answer. "Nay, it only brought us closer together and made us stronger."

"Clarissa needs more than just promises."

"Nicholas, darling, ye have known Alexander all your life. Do ye really think he willna do everything in his power to ensure she has what she needs? Look at everything he is doing to right the wrongs his brother did?"

"I suppose ye are right," he admitted begrudgingly.

She lifted on her toes and gave him a peck on his cheek, her hand patting him on the chest. "Love will always find a way, Nicholas. It did with us, and it will with them as well."

She headed towards the hall, and Alexander scrambled back as quickly and quietly as he could and then turned as if he were just entering the hall when she appeared in the doorway.

"Ah, Your Grace," she dipped her head in greeting. "I believe Nicholas would like a word with ye. He is waiting for ye in the drawing room." She placed a hand on his arm and squeezed, the small gesture somehow making him feel as if everything was going to work out in his and Clarissa's benefit.

He could only hope that was true.

CHAPTER TWELVE

Aᴸᴇxᴀɴᴅᴇʀ ᴋɴᴏᴄᴋᴇᴅ ᴏɴ the drawing room door and Nicholas turned from the window, lines creasing his forehead.

He pointed towards the hallway. "Gwen told me ye wanted to speak to me?"

Nicholas rolled his eyes. "Did she now?"

Alexander shrugged. "Do ye want a drink?" He asked, trying to brush off the conversation he had just listened to.

They left the drawing room and made their way to the study. He headed straight for the side bar and poured them each a generous serving of whisky.

"Is it about the auction?" He asked innocently, handing Nicholas one of the glasses.

"What is your plan for my sister?"

Alexander choked on the sip he was in the middle of taking. Wracking coughs paining his chest and making his eyes water.

Once he finally was able to catch his breath, he eeked out, "Pardon?"

Nicholas sighed and slumped in one of the chairs near the hearth, sipping at his whisky. "Gwen has seen how ye two act when ye are together," he took another pull from his glass. "I have, as well," he confessed. "I dinna want to see her hurt, Alexander."

The pleading in his best friend's voice killed him.

"I ne'er would, Nicholas."

Nicholas nodded, as if finally believing him. "I ken. E'en if 'tis hard for me to admit. But I will state it now, if you e'er do, I will kill ye with my bare hands," he vowed, but a smile lifted the corners of his mouth.

"I would expect naught else, brother." They lifted their glasses in salute and downed the remaining liquid. "Now, about the auction. I havena heard from Finlay yet regarding the auctioneer. I hope to hear soon."

"We will get that bastard Kitt. He is going to find out the hard way he messed with the wrong family."

Alexander smiled at Nicholas's reference to family. They were after all.

They had been before the war, during the war, and after still. That was something that wouldn't change. Even if it was a bit rocky for a time.

As far as livestock auctions went, the turnout for the Campbell planned auction was fairly average.

Archibald Allen had agreed to host the auction and call the bids. More than certainly due to a nice purse promised by Finlay.

Finlay had not told him of such a cost, but Alexander kenned there was one involved. The man would not agree to such an endeavor for no compensation. And of course, his friend would not tell him about the cost due to his current circumstances. He appreciated that, but also felt like a leech for being in the situation in the first place. However, once he had his flock back and was making money again, he would pay back his friend ten-fold.

Nicholas, Malcolm, Gunn, and Finlay were all in attendance. Alexander scanned the room but did not see Kitt. Surely, he would put the sheep up for auction. The man didn't have a clue on how to care for them, so the sooner he got them off his lands, the better. Or at least that was what Alexander was thinking, but now that he didn't see him here, he was wondering if his thoughts were misdirected.

"What are ye thinking?" Malcolm asked as he leaned against the wall watching people settle into chairs and linger about. The auction was being held in one of the castle's outbuildings.

"I dinna see Kitt."

"I havena seen the livestock up for auction, but I canna imagine him no' putting them up."

Alexander sighed, pushing his hand through his hair. "I would like to think the same thing, but I am beginning to have my doubts. What if he doesna? Then what am I going to do?"

Malcolm clasped him on the shoulder. "He will. The plan is solid. Mayhap he sent a delegate. 'Twould make sense. If I were him, I wouldna want to show my face around here either," Malcolm said with a chuckle.

"Ye speak the truth on that," Finlay added from behind them.

Archibald banged his hammer on the podium that had been set up in the front of the room and a raised block.

The men turned their attention to the auctioneer and waited. Alexander's nerves were on edge. He felt fidgety. Nervous.

The first lot he had no interest in. Then it was a lot of hogs, chickens, piglets. It went on and on. Of course, he didn't bid on any of them. He had one sole purpose here, and it had not yet come up for bid.

He waited, and his impatience grew. What if the sod didn't list his flock? Would Archibald find it intrusive if he approached the podium and had a look at the lists?

"Easy, brother," Gunn warned. "Ye're tight as a fiddle and we can all see it. Dinna let him see ye want it so much."

Alexander looked around. "He is no' e'en here."

"Just because we canna see him doesna mean he doesna have some sort of presence here. We just have to be patient."

Alexander nodded stiffly, rolling his lips inward as yet another lot of hogs was announced. How many people were selling hogs for crying out loud?

"Sold!" The smack of Archibald's hammer was wearing on Alexander's nerves. "We have one final lot, a late entry."

Alexander snapped his head up and scanned the room, looking for Kitt. His hopes fell as he still didn't see him in attendance.

"I will start taking bids for this lot of three hundred prize-winning sheep."

"Those are mine," Alexander declared. A lot of the townsfolk kenned what he was trying to do. His sheep were well-known and none of them would bid against him on this. Or at least he hoped not. "One hundred pounds," Alexander stated above the crowd, who watched him curiously. He knew they were well aware of his brother's shortcomings. Christopher had been and remained an embarrassment, but he was still his brother and he still loved him. Even if he was the reason he found himself in his current situation.

Alexander held his breath, hoping no one would bid against him. It wouldn't be Kitt, since he wasn't here. And Alexander was certain ye werena allowed to bid on your own lot.

"One hundred and fifty pounds."

Alexander whipped his head around to the sound of the voice that called out. It was not Kitt, but it also wasn't anyone he recognized.

"Do ye ken who that is?" Finlay whispered.

"Nay. Do ye?"

Finlay shook his head.

"Do any of ye ken who that is?"

An echo of nays rose up from the group. "No one is taking my sheep," he whispered. "Two hundred pounds!" He called out.

"Three hundred pounds," the unknown man countered.

"Hell's teeth!" Alexander swore. The man was definitely not a local. Otherwise, he wouldn't be trying so hard to outbid the *duke* of said lands. "Four hundred pounds." Mayhap that would be enough of a jump to deter the man.

The man twirled the end of his brown mustache as he studied Alexander.

Alexander returned the look, his eyes narrowed as he assessed the man.

"Eight hundred pounds," the man called out with a sneer.

The crowd began to whisper amongst themselves as they watched the exchange.

"Bloody hell. The louse just doubled the bid." He pushed his hands through his hair, knowing what he had to do. "One thousand pounds."

Was the man laughing at him?

Alexander pushed off the wall, but Gunn grabbed his shoulder. "No' here, no' now. Keep your wits about ye. Dinna let him ken that he is getting to ye."

That was much easier said than done.

"One thousand, five hundred pounds."

Alexander felt his blood rush to his face as he fisted his hands. It would be satisfying to introduce the sod to his blows.

"Easy, remember the goal," Gunn said, his voice calm and even.

Taking a deep breath, "'Tis easy to say when 'tis no' your wallet." He looked towards Archibald. "Two thousand pounds."

The crowd's attention focused on him and then shifted to the moustached man in the back.

Archibald looked to the stranger, his brows raised in question. "Going once, twice—"

The man smirked, looked Alexander right in the eyes and called out, "Three thousand pounds."

Gasps went out from the crowd as their eyes volleyed between the two men.

The urge to jump the crowd and throttle the man continuously outbidding him was almost overwhelmingly strong. But no matter how much he wanted to do that, he couldn't.

He drew in a deep breath, his jaw clenched as he ground his teeth in anger.

"Four thousand pounds," he challenged.

"Going once," Archibald announced.

Alexander glared at the man, who finally put his hands up and shook his head, giving a sarcastic bow to Alexander before turning on his heel and leaving the auction.

"Sold to the Duke of Argyll for four thousand pounds."

Alexander paled. His sheep. They were once again his. But he didn't have four thousand pounds to give. He approached Archibald to pick up his pay ticket.

The auctioneer handed him a piece of paper instead. "The lister wanted to work with the winner personally. His address is inside."

Alexander flipped open the note and as expected, saw Kitt's name signed at the bottom. But he did not expect the note contained within.

We have much to discuss, Argyll. We shall speak soon.

He crushed the paper in his hands. "Bloody bastard," he spat.

"What is it?" Malcolm asked.

"He knew. He was playing a game the whole time."

"Who? What?"

"That bloody bastard set me up. He knew all along I was going to go to whatever lengths I could to win the bid. I am certain that man was a pawn in Kitt's game."

"How can ye be so certain?" Finlay asked.

He shoved the note to Finlay. "Because Archibald handed me this instead of the pay note.

THE WALLS OF Millwool castle seemed to close in around Clarissa. The men had been gone most of the day. She had wanted to go to the auction, but both Nicholas and Alexander insisted she stay here with Gwen.

So, instead of seeing what was happening, she only saw scenario after scenario running through her head about what *could* be happening.

She and Gwen sat in the parlor and waited for their return. She had tried to occupy her mind with a book, but it just sat closed on her lap. She couldn't concentrate on the pages every time she started to read, so she finally gave up and had taken to wringing her hands instead.

"Clarissa, ye must relax." Gwen said over the rim of her teacup.

She shoved the book aside and stood, moving to the window to see if the men were on their way back. "I canna, Gwen. My nerves are all on edge. What if Alexander doesna get this sheep back? What will happen to him? To Millwool? To his people? To his sheep?"

"Woah," Gwen set her cup and saucer on the table and joined her at the window and put an arm around her shoulders. "Ye are worrying overmuch on this. Alexander is too smart to let that wee troll win this."

Clarissa giggled at the nickname Gwen gave the American.

"He is a wee bit trollish, is he no'?"

Gwen squeezed her into a hug. "Aye, he is. And he isna worth us wasting time thinking or talking about him. Alexander is a powerful duke. He will win this battle easily."

She sighed, her eyes focused on the path that led to the outbuilding where the auction was being held. She couldn't see the building, but there had been people traveling the road all day.

"Come," Gwen urged, tugging gently on her arm. "Have some tea and we will wait for the men to return. They shall no' be much longer, I presume."

She took one last, long look at the path, and acquiesced.

"Nicholas and I saw ye and Alexander in the garden yesterday."

Clarissa's face flamed as her eyes shot to Gwen's.

"Ye seemed to be enjoying yourselves," she added with an impish smile.

A sudden lump had formed in her throat. Though Gwen was

well aware of her feelings for the Duke of Argyll, Clarissa's mind raced to the time she had spent with Alexander there. They had not kissed, regretfully, but also thankfully since they had been seen. But there were a few intimate moments.

Her cheeks set aflame as she tried to choose her words wisely. "Aye, I was going for a stroll in the garden, and he wanted to give me a formal tour. He caught me just as I was going out the door."

"Hmmm, seems quite coincidental, do ye no' think?" She asked innocently.

Clarissa shrugged, plucking at a piece of lint on her skirt. "I thought it was verra kind of him."

"Aye, I agree. Did ye like it?"

Her eyes shot to Gwen. "Like what?"

"The garden," she said, a brow lifted in amusement. "I mean, ye did say he was giving ye a formal tour, did ye no'?"

She nodded. "'Twas lovely."

"Hmph."

"Why are ye making that noise? Do ye no' believe me?"

"Och, aye. I believe ye. The garden is verra nice. Nicholas and I have strolled through it as well. But," she paused dramatically. "It did seem like more was going on when ye sat upon the bench."

"Ye saw us on the bench?" Clarissa's stomach dropped. Nicholas must be furious. Would he take it out on Alexander? Work against him in the auction? Surely not. That would be much too childish.

"Ye looked cozy."

Clarissa buried her face in her hands. "Oh no," she said through her palms.

Gwen joined her on the settee and clasped her hands. "Och, dinna fash. I believe Nicholas is seeing that ye two have genuine feelings for each other. Ye only need to give him time," she dropped her voice. "If I am being honest, I think he is having a hard time grasping the reality that his younger siblings are of marrying age. He doesna want to let ye go. Ye being the first just makes it that much harder."

Relief flooded through her at Gwen's words. Was Nicholas coming to terms with whatever was happening between her and Alexander? Could that even be possible? She could only hope. She wished her brother would see Alexander as she saw him. Strong, loyal, trustworthy. He had always seen him as a brother, and they had supported one another in the war. Now, her brother needed to support him at home.

Voices sounded below and Clarissa and Gwen shared a glance before jumping out of their seats and rushing downstairs.

Without thinking, Clarissa rushed to Alexander and clutched his hand in hers. "How did it go? Did ye get your sheep?"

Alexander looked at her, and then down at their entwined fingers, before meeting her gaze once again. Then his eyes shifted behind her and when she followed his gaze, her brother stood there, arms crossed, brows furrowed.

She snatched her hand from his, backing away. "I am sorry," she apologized. "I—"

CHAPTER THIRTEEN

ALEXANDER WANTED TO reach out and close Clarissa's hand in his but the look on Nicholas's face gave him pause and instead, he cleared his throat and stepped back himself.

Not wanting to embarrass her, he gave her a warm smile, hoping that she could see that he appreciated her gesture.

"I did indeed have the winning bid for my flock."

Clarissa clapped her hands together, a little bounce to her step. "That is great." Her gaze met his and she cocked her head to the side. "Why are you no' celebrating? This, above all else, is surely a cause for celebration. Is it no'?"

He grimaced. Did he want to tell her the whole story? Nay, he didn't. And he wouldn't. Not now. Mayhap not ever.

"'Tis naught for ye to fash over. I just need to meet with Kitt to pay my bid in person. But," he rubbed his palms together. "Right now I am famished. Anyone else?"

Confusion fluttered across her delicate features, darkening her eyes.

He tried to ignore the look, but it was so hard.

"Let me check in with Cook and see what she has available on short notice, and we can dine. Everyone, please gather in the dining room. I will join ye shortly."

He excused himself to find Cook, but Gunn stopped him with a hand on his shoulder. "Are ye all right, brother?"

That was a loaded question. One he didn't really have an answer for. He was thrilled he rightfully won the bidding.

Though he was pissed that the stranger in the auction forced the bids so high. On purpose, Alexander kenned. If he were a betting man, he would bet Millwool that the man was sent at the request of Kitt to drive up the price. It was common knowledge that without his sheep he had no income coming in other than his annual stipend, but that was far from being paid for the upcoming year and this year's payment had already been spent.

Or lost, rather, thanks to Christopher.

Alexander barked out a maniacal laugh. "Och, aye. Splendid. Thank ye for asking."

Gunn eyed him warily. "Ye dinna seem so."

"Really? Really? I have just lost thousands, I repeat, thousands to regain a flock of sheep that were rightfully mine to begin with."

Gunn clucked his tongue. "There was definitely something amiss about the bidding."

"Aye, I deduced that already. Somehow that man at the auction and Kitt were colluding. I dinna ken what his plan is, but I will get to the bottom of it. And that bastard will pay. Way more than the thousands I now owe him." He spun and stomped off towards the kitchen. "Bloody hell," he cursed to no one in particular.

As he neared the kitchen, he slowed his steps. He didn't want to scare off Cook by barging in there and demanding food. While the woman was more than accommodating, he would get a much better meal if he asked nicely.

The smell of baking bread and roasting venison assaulted his senses the closer he got. The smell was divine, and his stomach rumbled in want.

Cook was hunched over a table, mortar in hand as she pulverized some spices into a scrumptious seasoning, he was sure. She looked up as he entered and set the pestle down and wiped her hands on her apron.

"Your Grace, what can I get ye?" Her round face was red and her hair, just starting to gray, peaked out of the mobcap she wore.

But nonetheless, she gave him a warm smile.

"I ken ye are otherwise occupied, but would ye mind putting something together for everyone in the dining room? Do ye have anything ready? Finger sandwiches would be fine."

"I shall see what I have and get it to ye soon." She shooed him out of the kitchen. "Now, leave me alone and go entertain your guests."

"Thank ye. Ye are a gem."

"That is what they say. Dinna forget or ye may lose me to another estate," she jested.

"Ne'er. I willna let ye go." He laughed but turned to her once again. "Truly, Cook. Thank ye."

She waved her hands at him in a sweeping motion. "Go now, Your Grace, before ye make me blush."

In a better mood than he had been just a few minutes before, he thought of Clarissa as he went to meet everyone in the dining room. The way she had run up to him when he walked in the door, concern creasing her forehead, hit him like a gut punch. But when she reached out and clasped his hand? That was the best feeling. It was as if he had just returned home to his loving bride, and she could not wait to see him come back.

He stopped short, closing his eyes, and groaned. Bride. Love. What the hell was he thinking? He was closer to restoring his livelihood, but he had not yet. And Nicholas still appeared to be adamant that he leave Clarissa alone. Even after the talk they had had earlier.

In the dining room, tea had been served, and the chair at the head of the table had been left vacant for him. Normally, Christopher would be sitting at one of the chairs at either side of him, and one of his brothers would take up the others, but not tonight. For one, Christopher was gone. And hopefully not falling deeper into any gambling debts. But two, to his right, Clarissa sat sipping her tea and chatting with Gwen, who sat beside her.

Her gaze slid over to him, and she gave him a shy smile before returning her attention to Gwen and engaging in whatever discussion the two of them had ongoing.

"Cook will be along shortly with something small to fill our bellies until this evening's meal," Alexander announced, before sitting down and pouring himself a cup of tea. Not his beverage of choice, but he supposed he could not drink whisky all day and night.

James appeared and bent down to Alexander. "A missive has arrived for ye, Your Grace." He held out a tray containing the note, and Alexander accepted it.

"Thank ye, James."

With a bow, the butler left just as quietly as he had entered.

He pushed away from the table and moved away from the women's conversation. His friends, sensing that this was business, followed him over.

"What is it?" Finlay asked.

"Is it from Kitt?" Nicholas snarled.

By his reaction, Alexander could tell his best friend was ready to go to battle with the bastard. The thought brought a smile to his lips. He, too, would love to go to war with the louse.

Alexander broke the seal—a brown K—and read the note.

"Well. What does it say?" Gunn asked impatiently.

"He wants to meet. This eve. At his property."

Malcolm nodded. "We will join ye. A collective show of support."

Alexander shook his head. "Nay. Though I appreciate the offer. I believe he will perceive that as weakness. For a man of such small stature, he surely has an ego the size of the hemisphere."

"I dinna like that." Nicholas grumbled.

"Och, he willna attempt any such thing. He is no' calling me to his estate to harm me. Nay, he wants to discuss something. I will go—alone—and see what his terms are. There is no need for a group attack."

"'Twouldna be an attack."

"Pray tell, how do ye think he would perceive all of us marching up to his doorstep for a meeting that was supposed to only be between him and me?" He pulled at his cravat to loosen it and rolled his head from side to side. "I can do this alone."

CLARISSA TRIED TO concentrate on what Gwen was saying, but her attention was drawn to Alexander and the group of men on the far side of the room. Hunched together, they were speaking in low voices, and she could not hear what they were saying, no matter how much she strained her ears.

Gwen placed a hand over hers. "Clarissa?"

She gave Gwen a guilty look. "I am sorry. I am trying to—"

Gwen smiled, "Hear what the men are discussing?" She clucked her tongue. "'Tis rude to eavesdrop," she admonished teasingly as she leaned into Clarissa. "I bet ye if we stopped talking and focused, we could make out the conversation."

Clarissa's eyes widened with her sister-in-law's willingness to help her. With a devilish grin, Clarissa put her finger to her lips to silence them both and they listened intently. But it was to no avail. The words remained a secret.

When Alexander's gaze snapped to hers, she jumped. It felt as if he caught her doing something she was not supposed to do. Which, in a way, she surmised was true.

He nodded towards Nicholas and then the men returned to the table, but instead of taking his seat at the head of the table, Alexander announced that he would be taking his leave.

"I am sorry to leave ye all, especially since ye will be eating soon. 'Tis most rude of me, I ken, but there is an urgent business matter that I must attend to. I will check in on Cook afore I leave to ensure she will bring out the food shortly."

He paused by Clarissa, confliction creasing his brows. But whatever it was passed and with a brief nod, he spun on his heel and left the room.

"What do you suppose that was about?" Clarissa asked. She did not address any one in particular.

"I dinna ken," Gwen answered, gazing at Nicholas.

"'Tis regarding his sheep. He is going to talk with Kitt who insisted on a meeting at his estate."

"Is he in danger?" Clarissa asked quietly. Her mind suddenly conjuring up all kinds of unthinkable scenarios. What if he were to get hurt?

"Against that welp? Nay. Alexander can verra well handle himself."

"Ye let him go alone?"

Nicholas sighed. "Alexander is stubborn. We offered to go as well, but he wanted to do this on his own. He will be fine."

But even though she believed Nicholas's words, she couldn't help but think of all the ways things could go wrong. What if it was a trap? What if Kitt had some dastardly plan in place? Alexander was going there alone with no one to help if he ran into trouble. Oh dear. She started wringing her hands together. Her favorite pastime of late, it seemed.

"Dinna fash, sister. I assure ye, he will be fine."

"Let's go for a walk," Gwen offered, and Clarissa knew she was trying to take her mind away from Alexander, but just then, servants entered the room carrying trays of sandwiches and fruit.

Settling back into her seat, she reluctantly filled her plate, but no matter what she did or what conversation was going on around her, she couldn't stop thinking about Alexander and what was transpiring at the Kitt estate. Was he trying to convince Alexander once again to use her as a barter? She would rather be unmarried and a spinster than to be used as a pawn. She trusted Alexander wholeheartedly. But what if Kitt did something that left him no other choice?

What would he do then?

CHAPTER FOURTEEN

I T HAD BEEN a long time since Alexander had visited the Kitt estate. Back when his father was still alive and he and Christopher were teens. He didn't remember much of the details back then, but the estate that stood in front of him was surely worse for wear than afore.

The grass was unkempt, weeds climbed the walls and columns. The brick exterior of the house needed care. Pieces of brick and masonry had fallen or been worn away with time. The once whitewashed columns were now gray and dingy. The path that led up to the front of the estate was overrun with foliage that had crept onto the walkway, all but obscuring it from view.

Either Kitt couldn't afford the upkeep of the property, or he didn't care. Alexander assumed the latter considering how he wouldn't accept any monetary compensation for the sheep, barring tonight.

Alexander expected Kitt to demand payment right away, which he would have to hold him off for a bit until he could obtain the necessary funds. He didn't have them at this point in time.

A bleat sounded from the distance, the sound music to his ears. He was tempted to follow the call so that he could see how his flock fared, but the door opened and Kitt trilled his name.

"Ah, Your Grace," he dipped down dramatically, mocking the greeting. "Welcome to Kitt Manor."

Alexander ground his teeth, but otherwise ignored his irritation of the man, and tipped his hat at the louse. "Kitt. Ye summoned me."

"I did, yes. Please, do come in."

The man must definitely be low on funds if he didn't have a butler. Mayhap he didn't have time to hire one yet.

Inside, the state of the house did not fare much better than the outside. The musty smell assaulted Alexander's nostrils and he had to do everything in his power not to cover his nose with a gloved hand. The place was in dire need of a good cleaning. Dust covered everything, including the sheets still covering some of the furniture. The grimy draperies made the parlor, where Kitt had led him into, appear even darker. The faded wood could use another coat of stain to protect it and bring it back to its former glory.

"I apologize for the state of the house. My housekeeper has not arrived yet. I am eagerly waiting on her appearance."

Alexander said nothing as he waited for the man to get to the point.

"Sit, please." He pointed to a faded blue wing-backed chair that could very much use a date with the upholsterer.

But the sooner he acquiesced to whatever Kitt wanted, the sooner he would get this over with so he sat and couldn't stop the cough that erupted as dust kicked up and settled around him.

Kitt acted as if naught was amiss and sat in a chair on the opposite side of the unlit fireplace.

The chill in the room could be dispersed with a fire, but Kitt appeared to have no intention of getting one going.

"Ah," Kitt clapped his hands together. "Where are my manners? Would you like a drink? Brandy or cognac?"

Alexander thought about turning down the offer, imagining the state of the drink ware, but thought better of it and gave a quick nod. "Cognac, please."

Jumping to his feet, Kitt poured the drinks and after handing Alexander his glass, settled back into his chair.

"I feel as if we should toast."

Alexander lifted a questioning brow. "Whatever for?"

Kitt chuckled. "Right, right. You most certainly do not feel these are celebratory circumstances."

"Ye are correct." He had enough of small talk. He wanted to get back home to Millwool. Back to Clarissa. "Shall we get down to business?" he asked impatiently.

Clucking his tongue, Kitt wagged his finger in Alexander's direction. "So hasty, Your Grace."

"I do have other matters to attend to today."

Kitt sneered. "Ah, but none as important as this one, truly."

Alexander sighed. The cretin had him there and he knew it. Bastard.

He sipped his cognac, studying the liquid as he twirled it in his glass, drawing out the time.

The louse could use a good throttling and Alexander would be happy to be the one to give it. But he also knew that would not get him what he needed. He sat silently, waiting for Kitt to say whatever it was he had beckoned Alexander here for.

"Who knew that my flock of sheep would fetch such a price." His eyes met Alexander's. "It was quite the bidding war, I was told," he said with a smile.

Alexander ground his teeth. He didn't enjoy being goaded, especially by the likes of someone like Jacob Kitt, but he was between a rock and hard place. He quite literally was at Kitt's discretion.

"I myself was quite surprised at how much someone would pay for some sheep."

Hands fisted in his lap, he growled. "They are prize-winning sheep."

Kitt dismissed his statement with a wave of his small hand. "Still sheep, nonetheless. But the final price," he shook his head. "You were very determined, I will give you that."

"Ye ken I had no choice, but to pay whatever price was necessary to regain possession of my flock."

"Which brings me to why I invited you here this morn. "Just

how badly do you want your sheep?"

"I have already bid an extraordinary price. I believe that shows ye how badly I need them back."

Kitt stood and walked to the dirty window, gazing through grime to look upon the field. "You have. I also know you do not have the money you set forth in your bidding." He walked back to his chair and sat down. "Now, I consider myself a fair man."

Alexander couldn't stop himself from scoffing at that statement. In the short time he'd known the man, Kitt and fair had never crossed his mind in the same sentence.

Kitt lifted a brow, but otherwise ignored Alexander's reaction. "That being said, I think it only fair I give you seven days to pay your bid."

"Seven days? A week?" Alexander needed time, there was no question in that, but even he didn't think a week would be enough to be able to gather what he needed.

"I can see by your reaction that you are having your doubts about the timeline. I think it is more than generous considering that you are supposed to have the money in hand when bidding." He clucked his tongue in admonishment.

Alexander glared at him. "And *fair* people dinna send a lackey to the auction to drive the price up to an astronomical amount purposely."

Kitt clutched at his heart as if he had just been shot. "Truly, I am offended by such an accusation. Have you any proof that I did such a horrendous thing? I was not even in attendance for the auction."

Alexander snapped his mouth shut. It was only making things worse, and he didn't need that right now. He needed to keep his head on and not fall into Kitt's goading. That was exactly what he wanted.

"What is it ye want?"

"I thought I made myself perfectly clear. You have seven days."

"And if I canna come up with the money in that time?"

"Ah, yes," he rubbed his hands together. "If you do not have the money on my doorstep on the seventh day, I will kill one of your precious sheep. One a day until the debt is paid.

Alexander flew out of his chair and grasped the collar of Kitt's shirt. "Ye wouldna dare," he ground out.

Kitt tugged on Alexander's wrists. "Tsk, tsk. I would be very careful on how you handle yourself from this point on, Your Grace. You would not want word of your behavior to get out amongst the city. Or to let everyone know that you are unable to pay your debts. What kind of duke would that make you? Unable to care for your people." He shook his head, feigning disappointment.

"The sheep have done nothing to ye."

"That is true. However, I do not care for sheep. They're loud, bleating creatures. Annoying me at all times of the day and night. I would be happy to see them gone—one way or another."

The pit in Alexander's stomach grew. Kitt wasn't lying. The thought of losing even one of his flock was heartbreaking. They didn't deserve to be treated in such a manner. Despair settled over him. What was he going to do?

Kitt tilted his head to the side as he watched Alexander. "Of course, there is *one* more thing you could do."

Alexander held his breath, waiting for Kitt to continue, kenning that he was not going to like what was coming out of the bastard's mouth.

"You can have your precious sheep back without paying me one pence."

Alexander pierced him with a glare, having an idea where this conversation was leading.

"One night. One night is all I need. You arrange for the lovely Clarissa Gordon to spend the night with me and your debt to me will be forgiven. You get your sheep back and we all go on our merry ways.

"Ye are a vile man. She is not an object to barter with. She is a woman. Not chattel." His stomach churned at Kitt's disgusting offer.

"See," Kitt wagged a finger. "That is where you are wrong. Do you want your sheep back or not?"

"Not over Miss Gordon's integrity. I have no say over what she can and canna do. That is up to her brother."

"Ah, do not play coy with me, Your Grace. I have seen the way you look at the girl. Anyone near you can tell how much you care for her. And I call your bluff on her brother. The two of you are best friends are you not?"

"Ye canna be serious."

"Oh, yes. I am. Quite serious as a matter of fact. Ponder my offer, Your Grace, but do not take too long." He tapped his watch. "Tick Tock. You have less than a week."

"Ye will ne'er, e'er lay one single filthy finger of yours on Clarissa Gordon. Mark my words."

Kitt shrugged. "Then you best be pooling your resources. You have got a lot of money to pay up. Unless, of course, the sheep." His fingers made the shape of a pistol, and he held it up to his temple and pulled the trigger, laughing manically.

The bastard was insane. But Alexander fully believed that he would indeed start killing his sheep if he didn't get what he wanted. Without another word, he spun on his heel and walked out the door.

Outside, he paused and breathed in deep, listening for the sounds of his sheep. They must have wandered further away from the estate because he could no longer hear them.

"I promise I will get ye home," he vowed to the wind.

CLARISSA ANXIOUSLY AWAITED Alexander's return, but when he walked into the house, the tension rolling off his body was enough for her to not approach him and ask him how his meeting with Kitt went.

It was obvious that things did not go as planned.

The door slammed behind him, and he headed straight for his study.

She assumed he didn't get his sheep back. If he had, she would think his demeanor would be much more pleasant.

"Let's enjoy a cup of tea and let the men do whatever it is they need to do," Gwen said, coming up behind her. Nicholas was there too, though he continued on down the hall towards Alexander's study. "I think they have much to discuss." She looped her arm around Clarissa's and pulled her in the direction of the kitchen.

Clarissa was sick of tea. Every time something happened, she was told to enjoy a cup of tea and leave the men to their discussions. There had to be something she could do to help. Drinking tea was accomplishing naught. But what could she do?

Clarissa let Gwen lead her away. She was right, of course. There was naught she could do to help and would not even ken where to start if she did, no matter how much she wanted to.

"It appears things didna go well," she quipped, stating the obvious.

Gwen shrugged. "I dinna ken. But I am certain that Nicholas and Alexander will figure out what to do. They have a knack for getting what they want. Surely, this will be no different."

"Your Grace, Miss Gordon," Cook greeted them as they entered the kitchen. "Do ye need something?"

"Could we mayhap trouble ye for some tea?" Gwen asked.

Cook nodded and gave them a smile. "Aye, your grace, I can do that. Shall I bring it to the drawing room?" She suggested, not wanting the two of them hanging around the kitchen.

"That would be lovely. Thank ye," Gwen said and tugged on Clarissa's arm to follow her.

She would have much preferred to take tea in the library. Sitting on a chaise lounge with a hot cup of tea and a book in her lap sounded like the perfect way to spend the afternoon—and try to get Alexander off her mind.

"I see your brow furrowed in worry, Clarissa. Dinna fash. They will come up with a plan." She sat in one of the chairs and patted the one next to her for Clarissa to do the same.

"The auction was their plan and that did no' go as expected." She wrung her hands together. She didn't want to sit. Her nerves were frazzled. She was on edge, so she paced the floor.

"Ye canna do anything about it right now, dear Clarissa. Sit," she commanded gently.

"I dinna think I can. What is going to happen?"

Gwen shrugged. "Who can say? I most definitely canna. It really is up to Alexander to figure it out. And I am certain he will, especially with Nicholas's help. Plus, he has Gunn, Finlay, and Malcolm here to help even further. When all of them put their big, stubborn heads together, they can find a solution to any problem."

Clarissa couldn't help but laugh at Gwen's description of the men. "'Tis true. But it doesna lessen the worry I feel." She collapsed into the chair beside Gwen. "My concern is rising as the hours pass. Why is that?"

Gwen gave her a knowing smile and leaned closer. "I think ye ken the answer to that."

She studied her sister-in-law. The age difference between them was only a handful of years, but she seemed so much wiser than Clarissa. A lot of that was due to how quickly she had to grow up to care for her siblings. A situation Clarissa had thankfully never found herself in. She would be forever grateful to Nicholas for taking such good care of her and their siblings when papa had passed.

Yes, she took over the care of her siblings while Nicholas was away, but the situation was far different. They had the resources needed to provide for themselves. Gwen did not.

Alexander had not had the same hardships as she and her siblings had weathered, but he'd had his fair share of things he had to overcome. The loss of his mother at a very young age— she had died whilst giving birth to Christopher—and then later, the death of his father as well. But she imagined that the biggest thing for him to overcome was his brother, who went through life as though he hadn't a care in the world. Alexander had done his best, but when the person does not want to be helped and will not see reason, there is not much one can do.

Yet still, Clarissa saw the way Alexander fought—for his estate, his people, even for his brother—failure was not in his vocabulary.

It was one of the qualities she admired most about the man. Of course, his dashing looks and muscular frame added to that.

She felt her cheeks flame and she brought her hands up to cup her cheeks.

Gwen raised her brows at her, a smirk tilting the corner of her mouth up.

Clarissa sighed. Gwen did indeed ken her too well. She was falling in love with Alexander Campbell. Her brother would be furious, but she believed Gwen would be happy for her. Lord knew, she already suspected as much anyhow.

"Surely, they will be out soon. Mayhap, we can invite them in for a cup of tea as well?" Gwen said over the rim of her teacup. "Alexander especially must be parched after his visit earlier."

"I dinna doubt that, but I also dinna doubt that the whisky is flowing quite freely in Alexander's study," Clarissa quipped. Plus, she had noted his aversion to tea during their stay. It was near the bottom of his list of drinks to partake in.

"Ah, ye may be correct on that front. Still, I would wager that if ye offered Alexander a cup of tea when he emerges from his study, he would certainly take ye up on it."

Would he? She wanted to believe he would.

"Well, why dinna we find out?" She nodded towards the drawing room door and the men's voices in the hallway filled the air.

"I canna."

"Pfft," Gwen dismissed her with a wave of her hand. "Dinna fash about your brother. I will deal with him."

Clarissa was sure she would. Gwen had a way of wrapping Nicholas around her pinky, and he would do her bidding no matter what she asked of him.

"I have a better idea than tea." A twinkle darkened her eyes and Clarissa could only imagine what activity she had conjured up. "Nicholas, darling," she called out as the group of men neared the drawing room doors.

He entered, a broad smile breaking out on his face as his eyes met Gwen's.

"Aye, love?" He bent and kissed her cheek.

"'Tis such a lovely day outside. Why dinna we promenade? Alexander and Clarissa can join us."

"I dinna think that is the best of ideas, love. Alexander's mind is a bit pre-occupied at the moment.

Clarissa's head snapped up and met Gwen's gaze. The woman knew exactly what she was doing. And from the look on Nicholas's face, he was onto her scheme as well.

"All the more reason for Alexander to promenade, then. The fresh air will help to take his mind off of things."

Nicholas sighed in defeat, knowing that somehow, some way, Gwen was going to get what she wanted. He could never deny her.

"Or maybe Alexander has some pressing matters he needs to attend to," Nicholas pushed.

Alexander poked his head in the door. "Did I hear my name?" he asked curiously.

"Aye. Gwen would like to promenade."

"Lovely. 'Tis the perfect time of day for such a venture. Ye will enjoy it." He turned to continue down the hall, but Nicholas called him back.

"Alexander, it appears that this shall be a double promenade."

Alexander's brows furrowed in confusion. "Pardon?"

"Dinna play daft. Clarissa will be joining us on our promenade. Ye should as well and escort her."

He cleared his throat. "Me? Ye want me to..." He let the

words fall away as his eyes bounced from Nicholas to her.

Clarissa thought her cheeks flamed before but now they were surely on fire. This was so embarrassing. Gwen was so direct in stating what she wanted. And surprisingly so, Nicholas did not put up a fight. Was he actually supporting Gwen's suggestion?

"Come along, ladies. Let us enjoy the day." Nicholas held out his arm for Gwen to slip hers into the crook of his elbow.

Alexander stood frozen in his spot, and Clarissa remained seated, her eyes darting back and forth between them and wondering if she was dreaming.

"We havena got all day, Clarissa," Nicholas said impatiently. "Alexander, do be a gentleman and see to my sister."

That seemed to snap Alexander out of whatever it was that had him rooted to the floor, and after one last look at Nicholas, he grinned at Clarissa and offered her his elbow.

She returned a shy smile as she accepted his proffered arm.

"I dinna ken what is happening with your brother," he leaned close and whispered. "But I willna let the moment pass."

"I understand if ye dinna have time."

A look of frustration marred his features, but he quickly masked it and gave her a pleasant smile. "Those matters arena going anywhere. I can deal with them later. As Nicholas said, we've an afternoon to enjoy."

His smile didn't quite reach his eyes, and Clarissa knew the worry he was feeling. It was truly unfair of her to occupy his time when he could be putting it to better use.

Alexander read her worry as hesitation and he pulled back. "If ye would rather no' promenade, I understand."

"Nay," she called, a little too quickly. "'Tis no' that. I ken ye have more important things on your mind. I dinna want to take ye away from that."

His shoulders relaxed and he gave her a genuine smile, one that reached his eyes this time. "Trust me, I will enjoy this much more than the tasks I need to do later."

CHAPTER FIFTEEN

C LARISSA'S HAND RESTED in the crook of Alexander's arm as they made their way to the square to promenade. The contact sending jolts of warmth through him that he found hard to ignore. Behind them, he could feel Nicholas's eyes boring into his back as he strolled with Gwen, watching his every move.

What did Nicholas think he was going to do? They weren't the only couples promenading and he and Clarissa were not promised to each other. He refused to do anything that would compromise her in any way. Not in such a public place anyway. He was well aware that if they had been caught previously, they would have been surrounded in scandal.

He had done his fair share of ruining lasses for marriage, but he was not that man anymore.

"I thank ye for accompanying me," Clarissa said quietly.

"Of course. It has been quite some time since I have promenaded and ne'er with such a beautiful lass."

She ducked her head shyly, trying to hide the pink tinging her cheeks.

A lass and her mother passed them, the girl meeting his eyes and fluttering her lashes. Did these lasses never cease in their constant search for a suitable husband? Apparently, his reputation wasn't as widespread as he thought. If it was, they would well know he was most definitely not suitable. Not wanting to encourage the lass, he just dipped his head in greeting and carried on. Being a single duke was exhausting when it came to the fairer sex. The constant attention, of which there was plenty—whether he wanted it or not, was off-putting. Now he knew how Nicholas felt when his mother played matchmaker.

With his mother long passed, that was one thing he didn't need to concern himself with. Though, admittedly, he would enjoy having his mother here. He was young when she died giving birth to Christopher and over the years the image of her face had faded more and more. Her painting hung in Millwool's hall but, even so, it was no replacement for being there. He missed her dearly.

"I ken 'tis no' my place to e'en ask, but how did things go this morn? With Baron Kitt?" Her voice was low as she spoke.

Clarissa's question pulled him back to the present. Grinding his teeth, his eyes fixed onto the walking path in front of them. The very thought of Kitt set his blood on fire. The nerve of the cretin to spew the threats he had. He had huge bollocks to do so. Of course, he couldn't speak such crude words to Clarissa, so he pondered his response before answering.

"He stated his terms, but no agreement was made."

She frowned. "So, ye willna be taking possession of your sheep?" Her eyes darkened.

"Och, I will. I can promise ye that. I just need to work out some logistics afore I do."

Nodding, she continued walking, pointing to a duck on the shore of the pond they passed. Laughing as the male joined his partner and they waddled away together.

"I am glad ye are getting them back."

He nodded curtly. "Thank ye. 'Twill take some time, but I will be verra happy when they are once again on Campbell lands." He glanced down at her. Her blue bonnet covered her curls that fell loosely to frame her porcelain skin. Her beauty took his breath away and he kicked himself for not noticing it sooner. But she was young and that wouldn't have been right, so he dismissed the thought. What was important was the here and now. And now?

Now there was no denying her beauty, even if she didn't realize how beautiful she was. He'd climb to the highest peak of Castle Millwool and shout it from the rooftops until she didn't question it.

"Alexander, Clarissa," Nicholas called from behind them. "Are ye ready to return?" Nicholas pierced him with a look, eyebrows raised. "I believe we have pressing matters to attend."

Alexander sighed. Nicholas was right, of course, but he didn't want to end the walk. He dipped down and whispered to Clarissa. "What do ye think? Should we listen to your brother or go rogue?"

Twinkling eyes, filled with mirth, met his. "I would verra much like that," she stated as she looked over her shoulder to her brother. "But I fear we willna help our cause to defy my brother at this time. I think we should be thankful he allowed this promenade at all, considering how against a match between us he has been."

Covering her hand that was tucked into the crook of his arm, he smiled. "Ye are right. 'Tis best if we dinna push him."

The smile she blessed him with nearly brought him to his knees. What he would give to be the receiver of that smile every day. He would be the happiest man on earth.

As they walked back to Millwool, Alexander let his mind wander to a future he wanted to manifest. A future with the lass currently at his side.

To say he was infatuated was an understatement.

CHAPTER SIXTEEN

After the time they had spent promenading, Clarissa retired to her room for a short rest. Her stomach swirled with unfamiliar feelings whenever she thought of Alexander. Whenever he was close, her flesh broke out in goosebumps, and warmth flooded her body. An entirely new feeling and, even though she and Gwen were close, she didn't dare ask about such things.

Unable to relax, and not wanting to pace the length of the room, she decided on a visit to the library so she could get something to occupy her mind and stop the wicked images that flashed whenever she closed her eyes.

She had had a taste of Alexander's lips, but she wanted more. Her stomach tugged at the thought. She wanted to feel his mouth on hers again. On her neck, lower, dare she say on her breast?

"Stop, Clarissa," she muttered in the room. Stopping in front of the mirror, she glanced at her reflection. Her skin was flushed, and she tried fanning herself, but the move did naught to stop her simmering nerves. Tossing her fan onto the vanity, she left the room and headed towards the library.

As she made her way down the hall, nearing the study, she could hear the men's voices. Alexander was speaking, and she slowed, making her steps as light as possible.

Knowing she shouldn't listen to their private conversation didn't deter her from pausing just outside the door. Looking from side to side to ensure she was alone in the corridor, she tilted her head in the direction of the study, placing her ear against the door and listened.

"…the bastard says he will start killing my sheep, one a day, unless I give in to his terms."

She clamped her hand over her mouth to stifle her cry. Baron Kitt was threatening the worst of actions.

He wouldn't. Would he?

She thought of the type of man Baron Kitt was and from her encounters with him, though they were few, she could see him saying such a thing. How awful.

"He is insistent upon spending a night with Clarissa," he spat. "'Tis disgusting. The man has no class."

"I will kill him." This time it was Nicholas speaking up.

"I will do that myself. But there is a way. The bank didna outright deny my request. They want Castle Millwool as collateral. That is what I will do."

Clarissa sucked in a breath. He cannot be thinking to do that. What will happen if Kitt goes against his word, and he refuses to give Alexander his sheep back? Or if something else happens and he can't pay back the bank note? Then he would lose Millwool.

She backed slowly away from the door, shaking her head. Nay, she would not allow that to happen. If all she had to do was visit Baron Kitt for a day, as unpleasant as the thought of that was, she would do it to save Alexander and his people.

How bad could it be? It was just one day. She thought of Kitt and how uncomfortable he had made her feel at the ball and swallowed down the lump that began forming in her throat. It didn't matter. All that mattered was Alexander.

The library forgotten, she made her way back to her room, a plan forming in her mind.

CHAPTER SEVENTEEN

CLARISSA'S HEART DROPPED. She would not be the cause of Alexander losing all that he held dear. If Jacob Kitt wanted her to spend time with him, then she would do so. She had not heard of either Alexander or Nicholas mentioning a deadline.

She had heard whisperings that Alexander had visited the bank to try to garner the funds needed to pay off his bid but didn't ken the outcome. Hearing him say that he would need to use Castle Millwool as collateral to secure the loan was something that she was against. What if something went awry and he couldn't pay back the money? His home would be turned over to the bank.

As duke he would be ruined.

It was a horrible situation to be in and Clarissa did not wish that on Alexander in any way. But she had just overheard Alexander and Nicholas's conversation. To save her, Alexander was willing to put his whole livelihood in the bank's possession.

She would not allow it. For once in her life, she knew the solution and planned to take matters into her own hands. Making her way up to her bedroom, she dug out a piece of parchment and quickly scribbled a note to Jacob Kitt, agreeing to his terms. But she would have to be careful of her movements. If Alexander even had a hint of suspicion of what she was doing, he would stop her before she could carry out her plan.

To not raise any suspicions, she added instructions to have his coachman wait on a nearby road and she would meet them there.

Tomorrow morning at nine.

Signing the letter, she sealed it and sought out one of the housemaids, and after making her promise discretion, gave her the missive to deliver to the Kitt estate.

Naught else could be done but for her to wait. On the morrow, she would give Kitt what he wanted—a day with her—and then be done with it. Alexander would get his sheep back and then they could move forward. Nicholas could no longer deny that Alexander was unable to provide for her as needed since Alexander would have his livelihood back.

All will be well. And finally, finally, she and Alexander would be together.

As she retired for the night and laid down in bed, pulling the soft duvet up to her chin, visions of her and Alexander together danced in her mind. She pictured how happy and thankful he would be to her. He would propose and they would have a grand wedding.

She fell asleep with a smile on her lips and Alexander's handsome face behind her lids.

"WHAT IS YOUR planned course of action?" Malcolm asked as the friends gathered in Alexander's study.

Alexander regarded his friend, shame settling on him like a cloak. He should not be having these discussions. He should never have been in this situation. *Damn ye, Christopher,* he thought.

He pushed his hands through his hair. "I am embarrassed to make such a confession, but as I dinna have the funds needed, I have naught choice but to go to the bank and offer up Millwool as collateral."

The multiple intakes of breath from each of his friends hit him like straight shots to the gut.

"Are ye sure, brother?" Nicholas asked, concern etched across his face.

Alexander nodded. "Aye. I willna allow that bloody American to lay a single fecking hand on Clarissa. No' now. No' e'er. Nor will he harm my flock. If he thought his threats to start killing my sheep would have me agreeing to his terms regarding Clarissa, he is sorely mistaken. I will see the ground run with his blood before such a thing happens." He pushed up from his chair and paced the floor of his study. "If 'tis Millwool that will get me out of this predicament, then I will do just that."

"Just how much do we ken about this Kitt fellow?" Malcolm asked, rubbing his chin.

"No' much," Alexander answered. "I am no' e'en certain when he arrived on British soil."

"Is anyone aware of what he did in America? His position there. His job."

Alexander shook his head. "Nay. I have naught idea of those things." He paused in front of the window and leaned on the sill, his gaze roaming over the fields in the distance that used to be occupied with his sheep. "Judging by how he has interacted here since he has made himself known, I am going to wager a guess that he was just as conniving in America as he is here."

"I would say that is a fair conclusion," Finlay added. "One doesna suddenly become pond scum. I think if ye," he dipped his head in Malcolm's direction, "looked into his past, ye would uncover more of the same type of schemes."

"Aye. I agree with ye, Finlay," Malcolm murmured. "I will see what I can uncover about him."

Alexander nodded. "Thank ye. Though it does me no good at this point in time. Whatever ye may uncover willna help me in my current situation. There just isna enough time."

"All right, back to the bank. Are ye certain they will give ye what ye need and in time?" Nicholas asked, concern creasing his brows.

"Aye. When I spoke with them, they stated as long as I offered up Millwool as collateral that there would be no issue and I would receive funding without pause. That is what I will do."

"I am no' sure that is the proper course of action," Gunn interjected.

"Why no'?"

"Millwool is your livelihood. If ye lose it, ye let your people down. What will happen to them?"

He began pacing again. "If I dinna offer it up as collateral, we will all find ourselves in the slums anyhow. I need my sheep to keep Millwool running. They're our main source of income. I have full confidence that once I have them back, I will be able to pay off the bank note within a couple of years' time. And in doing so, no harm will come to Clarissa or my flock. All will be well. We will just need to figure out a way to get Kitt to return to America. I will be damned if I have to see him show his face around here after what he has done."

"Ye are certain ye will be able to return the bank's funds?" Nicholas asked.

"One hundred percent." But even as he said the words his mind ticked through the numbers and how much wool he would need to sell to repay the note along with the income needed to provide for his people.

Malcolm stood. "I shall poke about in town. See what I can find out about the louse in the short-term. Someone has to have information."

Alexander nodded. "Thank ye. I will get my affairs in order today and will go to the bank first thing in the morn. The funds should be in my hands the day after and then we can take care of Kitt."

"Mayhap we can show him what happens when he comes to Scotland and tries to weasel his way into society," Gunn suggested, grinding his fist into his palm.

The friends chuckled.

"I am no' sure those lengths will be necessary."

Gunn looked disappointed.

"But we can ne'er ken what lengths may need to be taken," Alexander quickly added.

Nicholas stood and moved towards the door. "If we are done here, brothers, I must go to my wife."

"Och, certainly."

The friends hooted and hollered in jest.

"Ye lot are uncouth. My wife wants to stroll the gardens. I promised her I would."

Nicholas's love of gardens was known to all, but Alexander believed it was the company of Gwen that would hold Nicholas's attention and not the flowers and shrubbery of Millwool's gardens.

"Enjoy your walk."

"I shall take my leave as well," Malcolm spoke up.

"Care for some company whilst ye do your digging, Malcolm?" Finlay asked.

"If ye like. Just let me do the talking."

Everyone exited the study and scattered into different directions. Alexander looked around the corridor, empty now that his friends had departed. He wanted to go find Clarissa, bury his head in her neck and forget about all his troubles. To seek comfort in her arms. He exhaled loudly into the empty space.

The things he wanted to share with her, do with her. Until he had his livelihood back, they were all just distant dreams that he had no right wanting. But his heart had other ideas. No matter how much he told himself that Nicholas would never allow a union between them, visions of her on their wedding day, their wedding night, her pale skin flushed as she lay beneath him, later visions of her belly, round with their child—all those images flooded his mind.

He smacked the wall, trying to clear his head and headed back into his study, pulling his books from the drawer and slumping into his chair to go over Millwool's numbers for the umpteenth time, knowing they had not changed from the last time he had done so.

A vision of Clarissa laid out on his desk before him had him pushing back from his books and heading to fill his glass with the strongest whisky he had. Quickly, he knocked back the amber liquid, letting the burn warm his throat and chest as he refilled his glass.

He was certain Clarissa felt the same way he did. She had alluded to it on multiple occasions and the promenade that Gwen slyly arranged between them solidified it.

They only needed to convince Nicholas that his sister would be safe in Alexander's arms. Surely, his best friend must realize by now that he would never do anything to put her in harm's way. He had vowed as such on multiple occasions. And once he had his sheep back, his income would no longer be in question, so he would be able to provide Clarissa a stable life deserving of her station. She would be a duchess after all.

Clarissa Campbell, Duchess of Argyll. He smiled as the title rolled off his tongue.

He liked the sound of that.

CHAPTER EIGHTEEN

THE AIR WAS cool as Clarissa snuck quietly out of Castle Millwool and walked down the drive. She kept looking over her shoulder, worried that someone would take notice and come after her. She pulled her cloak closer and turned onto the street, hurrying towards where, hopefully, Kitt's carriage would be waiting.

The birds were unusually quiet as if they, too, were uneasy with her plan.

She had to admit her nerves were on edge. All night, she tossed and turned thinking about what the day would bring. But in the end, every scenario she conjured up in her mind was dismissed with the fact that in the end, Alexander would be whole again. She could handle dinner with Kitt. She'd been present at plenty of dinners of which were no interest to her. She could attend one more.

For Alexander, she felt like she could do anything.

She *would* do anything.

A couple walked along the street, arm in arm, chatting happily as they passed. Clarissa didn't recognize them and didn't make eye contact as they passed. They could be acquaintances of Alexander, or even her brother for that matter.

Turning the corner, she spotted a Phaeton stopped, a coachman waiting by the door. She paused, smoothing her skirt with gloved hands. Her heart pounded a steady rhythm in her chest. Her pulse quickened and for the first time she pondered whether or not she was doing the right thing.

Was she being naïve in thinking that Kitt had only honorable intentions in mind?

She didn't know much about Jacob Kitt other than what she had heard Alexander and Nicholas speak. And of course, she had met him at the ball they had all attended and had danced with him. It wasn't a pleasant dance and Alexander had saved her from having to suffer through another one, but they wouldn't be dancing at his house surely.

Nay, she imagined the man would host a dinner and they would converse.

How that would result in Alexander not having to pay his auction bid, she had no idea. It seemed hardly a comparative offer. She was nothing special. And as has been shown, she had no say whatsoever in the direction her life took. Everything was up to Nicholas, and if Kitt wasn't in Nicholas's good graces, then naught would come to fruition.

Taking in a deep breath, she slowly blew out through her nose, trying to calm her nerves and then repeated the process, before stepping forward and approaching the coachman.

"Miss Gordon?" The coachman moved away from the door and greeted her.

"Aye," she dropped into a curtsy.

"Baron Kitt has sent me to bring you to his estate as requested." He swung open the door and dropped the step. "Please, let me assist ye." He held out his hand and she accepted it and stepped into the carriage.

The door shut with a bang, and she jumped, startled as she settled onto the bench. She glanced out the window in the direction that she had come in to make sure no one had followed her. The street was empty, and she relaxed a wee bit as the carriage started to roll down the street.

Not knowing where the Kitt estate was she had not the faintest idea how long it would take to arrive. As the time passed, her mind wandered, and her nervousness rose. So much so, that the further they got away from Millwool, the more she was doubting her decision.

Nicholas would be furious once he discovered that she had left. And no one was aware of her intended destination. What if something went wrong? What if Kitt had ulterior motives? She had not thought of that possibility afore, but now could see where she could be walking into a dangerous situation.

All she wanted was to help Alexander.

Now she feared that her desperation to help him may have blinded her to the danger of what could happen.

Moving to the bench on the front side of the carriage, she knocked on the wall to catch the coachman's attention. It took a few minutes before he finally answered.

"Aye, Miss Gordon?" The man called.

"I apologize for the inconvenience, but I would verra much like to return to Castle Millwool."

The coachman was silent.

"Sir?" She called out a little louder, a tinge of desperation making her voice rise.

"Aye, Miss. Baron Kitt has given explicit orders. I canna turn back. I am to deliver ye as promised."

As promised? She wouldn't necessarily say she promised him anything, other than agreeing to his terms of spending the day with him. Surely, they could reschedule with no issues.

Though the timeline would be an issue. She had heard Kitt's threat to start killing Alexander's sheep if he didn't get what he wanted. And there were only two days left until his threats could come true.

He was a vile man if he thought taking his frustrations out on poor, innocent animals was the acceptable path to get what he wanted. Clarissa couldn't get the image out of her head. Both of the poor sheep and of Alexander's distress at seeing something he cared the world for being destroyed.

Alexander would see it as his own failings, even though that was so far from the truth.

Fine. She would meet with Kitt as she previously arranged. But she would need to be aware of her surroundings. The closer she got, the more she realized the man was completely untrustworthy.

When the carriage finally ground to a halt, Clarissa's heart jumped. She remained glued to the bench as the coachman opened the door and set out the step.

"Miss Gordon," he held out his hand to assist her out of the phaeton, but she remained sitting, making no move to leave the safe confines of the carriage.

All her senses told her to stay seated. Danger awaited her inside. She had never been one to believe in the mystical forces that warned of upcoming peril. But that was what she was feeling currently. A small voice telling her not to enter the estate.

"Miss Gordon," the coachman urged, extending his hand even further. "Baron Kitt is anxiously awaiting your arrival. Ye must no' make him wait any longer."

Her mind raced, trying to come up with a scenario that would get her out of this situation. But none came to mind. She couldn't rush out of the carriage, the coachman was right there and even if she managed to push him aside, he looked to be a strong man that was more than capable of chasing her down if she did escape him for the briefest of moments.

She squeezed her eyes shut. What had she done? With no choice but to go along with what had already been set in motion, she ignored the coachman's hand and grasped the outside of the carriage for balance and exited, stepping onto the muddy ground. She lifted her skirt to try to keep the dirt away, but it was no use as her shoes sunk into the wet earth.

Pausing, she looked at the estate looming before her. Unlike Castle Millwool, the Kitt estate was not welcoming in any way whatsoever. If she had not been brought here and happened upon the manor on her own, she would think the place had been abandoned. It was that unkempt.

She shivered, just imagining what the inside looked like. With a final glance over her shoulder, as if hoping that someone had followed her and would make their presence known before, she climbed the steps and walked into the foreboding building. But no one was there, and out of options, she moved forward.

The door swung open as she approached and Kitt stood in the doorway, a sneer on his lips. His brown hair was slicked off his forehead, making it look greasy, and Clarissa tried to hide her grimace.

"Miss Gordon. I am so glad you reached out." He stepped aside, allowing her to pass and enter the house.

She paused at the doorway and glanced around the small foyer. Much like the outside, it wasn't cared for properly. She could see how, when the former Baron Kitt lived here, the estate would have been impressive, despite its small size. Hints of grandeur were noticeable if you looked beyond the grime, dust, peeling paint, and faded wallpaper.

Remaining silent, her hands folded in front of her, she focused on not wringing them together and giving away how nervous she was.

"Please," Kitt said as he shut the door swiftly behind her, essentially locking them in the house together. "We can settle into the parlor for now." He waved his hand in the direction of the hall, and she moved forward towards where he pointed.

"I must say I was quite surprised at your message. It was most definitely not something I was expecting. Especially after the Duke of Argyll had so vehemently denied my request."

Clarissa sighed. "Aye, sometimes things change."

He narrowed his beady brown eyes and swept them up and down her body, causing a shiver to creep up her spine.

"Right. Well, glad I am of the change if I must confess." He opened a heavy door, the wood splintered on the edges. "Here we are."

Waiting for her to enter, he practically bounced from one foot to the other.

A sense of foreboding enveloped her. Being in his house alone with the man was bad enough. Did she really want to be confined to a small space with him? With no other choice, she moved forward. She had agreed to this meeting and now she needed to follow through with it, no matter how wrong she felt it was.

Inside the room, a small fire was lit, but yet it did naught to take the chill out of the air.

"Would you like a cup of tea? Please, sit. I will be right back with refreshments."

Was he making the tea himself? Other than the coachman who had brought her here, she had not seen any of his staff. Did he have any? If he did, she found it hard to believe they would let the house fall into such disrepair. How long had the estate stood empty, she wondered.

She studied the seats available. Two stuffed chairs were set on each side of the small fireplace. On the wooden mantel, mottled with pockmarks, a dusty vase held a bouquet of dead flowers. Unable to identify what type of flowers they were told her they had expired quite some time ago. She frowned, surprised that Kitt wouldn't have at least cleared those from the room before entertaining company.

A wing-backed chair sitting near a table seemed to be the best choice of the available options. There were no other chairs around it, so Kitt would need to keep his distance. Though she couldn't get herself to sit. She much preferred to stand.

Thinking about that, thank heavens they were not home at Huntly. Word would no doubt travel quickly that she had gone out alone and visited the home of an available bachelor. She shivered. To save her integrity, many would insist that they marry so as not to sully either of their names. She could not imagine such a fate. Or was that his plan?

"Ah, here we are." Kitt entered carrying an unpolished silver tray, the green verdigris prominent on the edges of the metal.

He picked up a white and blue china teapot. The spout was chipped and there was a crack in the belly of the pot that appeared to have been filled in. The grayish-colored spackle seemed to do the trick as no liquid escaped from damage.

"How do you take your tea, Miss Gordon?"

"Sugar and cream, if ye have it, please."

"Of course, I have sugar. Cream as well. What do you take me for? A pauper that cannot afford such luxuries?"

Surprised that he had any to offer her, she was taken aback. "Thank ye."

He dropped a sugar cube into her cup before holding up the small container of cream and poured a small amount and then looked at her in question.

She nodded and he set the pot of cream down.

He didn't pour himself a cup and she got a flash of danger thinking that he may have done something to the tea. Was it poisoned? Would he do such a thing?

Clarissa hadn't the faintest idea and once again, she cursed herself at the situation in which she now found herself embroiled.

Though, it would make no sense for him to poison her. Why say he wanted her here to then kill her? Nay, that scenario wasn't plausible.

She had heard Alexander mention Kitt was willing to barter for items other than money. Though as she looked around the decrepit room, the man was obviously in dire need of coin. What could possibly be more important to him than that?

"I am having a meal prepared for later. I do apologize that I do not have all my staff on board as of yet. But when I received your letter, I put out a call for a cook straightaway. Luckily, one was available and is currently working in the kitchen," he explained, his voice soft.

Was he trying to be charming? The smile he plastered on his face didn't reach his eyes and it seemed disingenuous.

"Sir Kitt—"

"Please, call me Jacob. We are, after all, beyond formalities."

She wasn't sure about that but did as he asked. "Jacob, 'tis no' my place to ask, I fear, but alas, I canna help myself. As ye ken, Alex—the Duke of Argyll," she quickly corrected, "cares verra much for his flock of sheep that ye are currently in possession of."

A look of annoyance crossed his face. "Yes, the sheep. Destructive critters, I must say. Eating up my grounds."

"Aye, I suppose they could be when one isna prepared for them. But are they well?" She asked, concern for their well-being weighing heavily on her shoulders. She did not want to be the cause for any of them to be harmed.

He scoffed. "The amount of bleating I hear continuously confirms to me that they are fine."

She scowled. That was no way to tell. They could be bleating because they are hurt, or lost, or for a plethora of other reasons. She wanted to see them for herself, so she prodded.

"Mayhap after tea we could stroll and visit them?"

"Visit them? You speak as if they are relatives you are checking in on."

She supposed in a sense they were. She just wanted to see them. That way she could let Alexander ken that they were safe.

Had Alexander realized she had left? Or Nicholas? It's possible they did not since they were more than certainly wrapped up in whatever plan they were trying to come up with.

She was happy that she could at least help Alexander. And prove to her brother that she was capable of making her own choices, and that included choosing her own husband.

The men may have not noticed she'd gone, but she would wager that Gwen had noticed. How long it would be before she alerted the others Clarissa hadn't the slightest clue.

HIS AFFAIRS CONCLUDED at the bank, Alexander drudgingly made his way back to Millwool. Mayhap he should gather his friends and head to the estate in Edinburgh. He shook his head. Nay, he needed to be here. The funds would be available to him in the morn, and he would then be able to pay Kitt his exorbitant fee.

'Twas extortion and they both knew it. But Kitt had him backed into a corner. There was no turning around now.

The carriage jerked to a halt in front of Millwool and he took a moment to compose himself before he exited.

Gunn met him at the door. "How did it go?"

Alexander sighed. "As well as it could when one was signing his livelihood away, I suppose."

Gunn gave him a curt nod, his mouth turned down into a frown. "I ken 'twas a verra hard step to take."

"Aye, 'twas. Though necessary. If ye'll excuse me. I dinna feel in the mood for talking."

He pushed past his friend and walked through the castle and out the back door. As he made his way down the steps that would take him to the gardens and then beyond that, the fields where his sheep had spent most of their lives, he once again cursed Christopher.

Did his brother realize the depths of destruction he had caused? Did he ken the steps that had to be taken so he could save their home? Their people?

He highly doubted it. The only thing Christopher cared about was himself and how he was going to afford the next game, whether it be cards or dice, it didn't matter. As long as he could feel the thrill of playing, he was happy.

It didn't matter that he was endangering everything their father had worked so hard for. His mind was beyond that. He was so selfish. Not caring about anyone but himself.

Gwen emerged from the hedged wall of the garden and smiled at him.

He gave her a quick wave, expecting Clarissa to pop out behind her, but she didn't.

"Are ye walking alone?" he asked, dancing around outright asking about Clarissa.

Gwen smiled knowingly.

She was sharp as a tack and saw right through his farce.

"I've actually no' seen Clarissa today. I assume she is curled up with a good book in her room."

He frowned. That didn't seem right. "Really?"

"Aye," she shrugged. "When I saw her last night afore we retired, she had seemed upset, but insisted it was naught. I dinna ken. Mayhap, she is homesick."

He clenched his jaw. "Mayhap. I suppose we will see her for dinner."

Brows raised, Gwen addressed him. "I suppose we will." She went to move around him, but paused, placing a hand on his arm. Her voice serious, she said, "I ken what Nicholas has told both ye and Clarissa, but I also see him watching the both of ye. He is no' blind to the chemistry between the two of ye." She patted his arm. "Give him time, he will come around."

With that, she left him standing there. He raised his eyes and glanced at the window that belonged to the room that Clarissa was staying in. He hoped to see her standing there, watching him, but the window was empty.

He sighed, sweeping his gaze over the landscape before turning around to head back inside. His plan was almost complete. Tomorrow, he would get the money to give to Kitt for his sheep. The thought of giving the bastard any money at all irritated him immensely, but once he was paid, he had no hold over them anymore. He would leave Clarissa alone, and hopefully disappear.

Disappearing was probably a bit much, but Alexander would be happy if he didn't have to ever lay eyes on Kitt again.

"THE MEAL WILL be ready for us to indulge in later." Kitt had moved to Clarissa's side, and she found herself cringing away from the man.

He had an off-putting scent to him. A cross between tobacco and body odor and she tried to breathe through her mouth when he was near.

"Would that be nice?" he asked when she didn't acknowledge his earlier statement.

Honestly, she just wanted him to step away, and when he didn't, she moved to the side, but was soon disappointed when he fell into step beside her once again.

Clearing her throat, she brought her handkerchief to her nose to feign a sneeze but took a deep breath behind the pleasant-smelling cloth, thankful she had tucked one into her reticule.

He lifted a brow in question but stepped away to give her space.

"Aye, dinner would be nice," she finally answered. She really didn't want to eat with him. Lord knew what kind of condition his kitchen was in. If it was in the same state as the rest of his house, the meal would leave much to be desired. That wasn't necessarily a bad thing. She didn't find she had much of an appetite in Baron Kitt's presence.

Had Alexander noticed she was gone yet? She couldn't help but wonder.

"Let us relax and enjoy some easy conversation."

She looked longingly towards the door, willing Alexander to burst through, but naught happened. She sighed and watched Jacob pick two pieces of small sandwiches from a plate that he had brought in with the tea.

He waited for her to take a seat and then took his own chair across from her and handed her the teacup, which was in the same condition as the pot. The handle of the cup had been broken off at one point and had been cemented back on. Small chips on one side of the cup gave the rim an uneven appearance and she avoided cutting her lips on the ragged edges by sipping from the other side.

After a few moments, he asked, "Is everything to your liking, Clarissa?"

She cringed at him calling her by her first name.

"I may call you Clarissa, can I not?"

"I would prefer if ye didna."

With a roll of his eyes, he sighed. "Fine. Miss Gordon," he drawled out her name sarcastically. "I do not understand how you Scots find such enjoyment in tea. I find myself much more inclined to coffee. Tea tastes so bland. I prefer the heartier taste of a coffee bean than a tea leaf."

She held her tongue, unsure if the question was rhetorical. She could not stand the taste of coffee. But she wasn't surprised that was his preference. She had heard that Americans preferred it over tea.

Jacob stared at her, waiting.

"Och, apologies. I thought ye were making a comment. It didna require an answer."

He just grunted and continued watching her drink with his beady brown eyes. His action made the hairs on Clarissa's arms go up. And for the umpteenth time since she'd left Millwool this morning she cursed her stupidity under her breath.

She wanted to escape these walls. They felt like they were closing in on her. Taking another sip of tea, she set the cup and saucer on the table. "Shall we go see the Campbell sheep now?"

"You were serious about seeing them?" He sounded dumb-founded at the idea.

"Aye." She looked out the dirty panes of the window. "Besides, 'tis such a lovely day it seems a shame to waste it being indoors. We willna have many more warm days until the air turns cold and we are forced to stay indoors."

"You Scots are an odd bunch. I had heard you were supposed to be a hardy lot. I think I will be able to handle the cold weather better than you all."

She doubted that, but once again held her tongue. She was only making excuses so she could get out of the house. Either way, she placated him with a forced giggle. "I believe ye may be right, Baron Kitt. I much prefer to spend the cold days near the warm glow of the fireplace." She didn't. She happened to enjoy the cold weather. The beauty of freshly fallen snow. The way it made the forest sparkle. But she would never admit that to him.

Nay. Baron Kitt would never know her likes and dislikes. She wanted him to know as little as possible about her. That was a vow she would keep.

"Very well," he said gruffly. "If you insist on seeing the sheep, we will do so." He stood and held out his hand to assist her up.

She was perfectly capable of standing up on her own, but knew Jacob's ego was fragile, so she swallowed hard and accepted his hand.

"Your shawl is in the other room. Let me fetch that for you and we can leave through the back door."

She nodded and watched him leave the room. Quickly, she glanced around, looking for anything that she could use as a weapon. She had a feeling that sooner or later, at some point before the night was through, she was going to need something to defend herself with against Jacob.

On the table, there was naught but a small teaspoon, the teacup and saucer, the platter of sandwiches, and the tea pot. There was the tray they were sitting upon, but it was too big for her to carry around and it would be too obvious what she was doing.

She needed to be discreet. She studied the room, but to her dismay, there was naught that would offer her any protection.

"Here you go." Jacob entered the room and placed the shawl on her shoulders, his fingers lingering a little too long.

She shuddered, and he mistook her disgust for a chill. "Are you sure you want to go outside? You are already shivering, and we have the fire here to keep us warm."

Her gaze swept to the waning flames of the fireplace. No one was keeping warm with that small blaze. And she certainly did not want him getting the idea that she wanted him to chase the chill away.

"I am certain. Please," she almost begged.

Thankfully, the man was oblivious to anything that didn't serve his purpose and he didn't note the plea in her voice.

With his hand at the small of her back, he pushed her forward to the opposite side of the room and out a door into a narrow hallway. The hallways were much smaller than those at Huntly or at Millwool. Also, opposite of those halls, this one was in desperate need of a coat of paint—just like the other rooms she had seen so far.

They exited the door and stepped out onto the grass. The edges of the blades starting to brown due to the time of year. There were no gardens at the back of the estate. No landscaping at all, really. It was just open meadows. No wonder why he let the sheep roam freely. They could essentially eat right up to the doorstep if they were so inclined.

"Let us head this way." He guided her left toward a well-worn footpath.

Warily looking around, Clarissa sighed when she saw that they were still alone. Nevertheless, she followed, knowing she couldn't do anything about it now. And he was taking her to the sheep, which was what she asked for. For that she was thankful.

The cool breeze loosened her hair from its bun, and she swept at the flyaway strands, tucking them behind her ear. As they neared a hill, she could hear the bleating of the sheep even though she couldn't yet see them.

An hour and a half later, Jacob was looking positively perturbed as she sat in the meadow, surrounded by Campbell sheep with a huge smile plastered on her face. They all looked well. They had been eating the resources provided by the land and Alexander would be happy to learn that they hadn't been sheared. Their woolly coats were still intact.

"Have you satisfied your curiosity, Miss Gordon?" Jacob shuffled from one foot to another.

"Aye. They look healthy."

He scoffed. "Why wouldn't they be?"

Clarissa shrugged. "Mayhap because ye have no experience in caring for such a flock. I was unsure what their fate may be."

He moved close to her, inhaling deep.

Did he just sniff her? She hid the shudder that threatened to rattle her whole body.

"Well, now that you are here, they will be returned to Campbell lands soon."

The louse didn't show the least bit of embarrassment at openly admitting that he had used her as a bargaining tool.

"That is, if things progress as promised."

She stepped away from him, a sense of foreboding enveloping her.

CHAPTER NINETEEN

A S EVERYONE GATHERED for dinner, Alexander waited impatiently for Clarissa to come down the stairs. Like Gwen had mentioned earlier, he also had not seen Clarissa all day. He at least thought he would see her as she went to the library to get another book to read or return the one she had been currently reading, but he hadn't.

'Twas possible she had brought several with her into her room. He told her she could take full advantage of whichever books she wanted, so it wasn't out of the realm of possibility. But he thought she would have emerged from her room at some point, if only to quench her thirst or for a meal.

As they all sat at the table waiting, they started to send questioning glances to each other.

Gwen pushed back from her chair and all the men stood. "I will go see what is keeping her," she said, placing a hand on Nicholas's chest, a worried frown on his face.

She left the dining hall and the men sat down. A maid came forward with a flask of wine and filled their glasses.

"Thank ye," Alexander said and fisted the glass most uncouth like and drank deep, forgetting his manners, and not caring that he did.

The men surrounding him were all in the war with him. They had seen the worst of each other along with the best. There were plenty of times when manners didn't play into their actions.

A few minutes later, Gwen reappeared, alone, her face pale.

"She is no' in her room," she blurted, approaching Nicholas, who stood up with such force it knocked his chair over.

"What?" he demanded.

Gwen shook her head. "Her room is empty."

"How is that e'en possible?" Alexander asked. "When is the last time ye saw her?"

"Last eve. As I mentioned to ye earlier."

Alexander glanced around the table at his friends. "Has anyone seen Clarissa today?"

They all looked at each other, shaking their heads. A chorus of nays echoing off the walls.

"Shite." He pushed his hands through his hair and stood, pacing the room. "If she is no' in her room, and she wasna with ye in the gardens earlier, Gwen, and no one has seen her, where can she possibly be?"

"I havena the slightest idea," Gwen said.

"Have ye checked the library?" he asked, knowing she wasn't there, but not willing to believe she could be anywhere else. He pushed open the door of the dining hall and took the stairs two at a time. Bursting through the library doors, not caring if he scared her, he glanced around the empty room. He couldn't imagine where else she would be in the castle.

"James!" He called out, descending the stairs.

The butler rounded the corner. "Your Grace?"

"Have ye seen Miss Gordon today?" He snapped.

"Nay, Your Grace."

A sense of foreboding crept under Alexander's skin.

"Gather the rest of the staff. Someone had to have seen her."

Ten minutes later, every person on the Campbell payroll stood in front of him as he paced back and forth.

"Has anyone seen Miss Gordon today?" He studied each person in front of him, his gaze stopping on the young maid that had been assigned to Clarissa.

Stopping in front of her, he tried to make eye contact, but the lass kept shifting her eyes everywhere but to his.

"Gretchen?"

"Aye, Your Grace," she curtsied.

"Do ye ken where Miss Gordon is?"

She sucked in her lip and bit it between her teeth.

"I need ye to tell me where she is," he hated the urgency that made his voice harsh.

The lass cowered a bit and took a step back.

"Tell me what ye ken, Gretchen," he demanded.

"She, M-miss Gordon made me promise no' to say anything, Your Grace."

He took a slow breath, trying to tamp down his anger. "Understood, but she may be in danger. Where has she gone?" He got a sick feeling in the pit of his stomach. Would she go there? He wanted to think she wouldn't. But where else could she possibly be?

The lass looked at him with fear in her eyes and he hated that he made her feel that way, but he couldn't be bothered with that right now. Clarissa was his priority.

Nicholas came up behind him, and made the poor lass cower even more. "Where is my sister?" he demanded, before Gwen pulled him back.

"Sh-sh-she has gone to the Kitt estate," the lass confessed quietly, tears sprouting in her eyes before she covered them with her hands.

Alexander's stomach dropped, his biggest fear come true. "Ready the horses," he snapped to the stable hand that stood near the end of the line of staff. "I will leave for Kitt's at once."

"No' alone, ye willna." Nicholas stepped forward.

"I will ride with ye, as well," Malcolm joined them.

"As will I," Finlay and Gunn said in unison.

Alexander looked around at his friends, thankful and proud of their unity. Their brotherhood.

"Ready five horses. Quickly," he commanded.

The boy nodded and rushed off to the stables, a couple of others following him to help.

Alexander could see naught but red. His anger simmered just below the surface. "If he has laid one fucking hand on Clarissa, I will skin him alive," he vowed.

CLARISSA SAT AWKWARDLY in the small dining room. Its faded wallpaper told stories of better days. The chipped dinnerware did the same. Jacob sat at the head of the table and had insisted that she sit beside him on his right.

She poked around at the meat, was it fowl? She couldn't tell. It had been severely overcooked, and it no longer resembled its former self. Jacob didn't seem to mind as he roughly sliced through the tough meat. His actions causing the whole table to shake. He popped a bite into his mouth and chewed loudly, his mouth wide open as he did so, bits of food escaping with each chomp.

His lack of manners didn't surprise her. She had expected as much. And while she didn't really eat the fare that had been set in front of her, she did take note of the knife she was given. Thinking it may come in handy later in the evening, she took advantage of Jacob's distraction and slipped the knife off the table and slid it into the sleeve of her gown.

She would need to move carefully as not to give it away.

"Is the food to your liking?" Jacob asked, his mouth full of the bite he'd just taken.

Her eyes met his as they bored into her. Pushing around the boiled potatoes, she nodded. What else could she say? Nay, the food is disgusting? She certainly could not. No matter how uncouth Jacob Kitt appeared, she could not stoop to his level. She had been taught manners, had gone to etiquette school. She wouldn't go so far as to eat, but she had full confidence in herself that she could maneuver the items on her plate in a way that would convince Jacob that she had eaten.

He wouldn't expect her to eat everything on her plate anyway. That would not be in the least bit proper.

After clearing his plate, he patted his stomach and belched loudly, the sound echoing off the room's faded walls.

Clarissa bit her tongue and hid her disgust.

"Are you finished?" Jacob leaned in and asked, his mouth close to her ear.

She shivered at the nearness and her stomach threatened to revolt at the stench.

He leered at her reaction, licking his lips.

"I am. Thank ye."

He draped his arm over the back of her chair, and she scooted forward, trying to escape his touch. "I think we should move to the salon. We can enjoy the fire," he said suggestively.

Clarissa slipped out of the chair, careful so that the knife stayed in place. She would not hold back on using it if the situation arose.

Jacob clapped his hands. When a servant appeared, he ordered the lass to bring a flask of wine. "None of that whisky that you all seem so fond of. No offense, but the taste doesn't sit well on my tongue. I much prefer wine."

Was the lass the same person that had cooked the meal? She had to assume she was.

He grabbed her hand and pulled her out of the dining room. "Come, we'll have wine in the salon."

ALEXANDER PUSHED HIS horse forward. With each minute that passed, his worry grew. How long had Clarissa been in Kitt's clutches? Had he harmed her? He clenched the reins, his knuckles white as his knees dug into the horse's sides, urging him to run faster.

"We will get her, Alexander." Gunn called out beside him, his voice barely registering over the sound of the horses' pounding hooves.

The images flashing in Alexander's mind were of every worst scenario that could possibly happen. After he confirmed that Clarissa was safe and hadn't been harmed, he was going to make sure she kenned how stupid of a move she had taken.

Mainly, he just wanted to ensure she was safe. What the hell was she thinking going to Kitt? Especially alone and not telling anyone.

The ride was ostensibly long. He didn't remember it taking this long when he had visited previously and that was when he traveled in his coach. A single horse should be able to make the journey in much less time, but time seemed to slow as they rode.

"Please, please be safe," he pleaded to the wind. He wasn't a religious man but found himself willing whatever powers to be that looked over the universe to also look over and protect Clarissa until he got there.

"Wine?"

"Nay, thank ye," Clarissa declined Jacob's offer.

He raised a brow in question.

Giving him what she hoped was a passable smile, she explained. "I must confess wine gives me the most horrid ache in my head." It was a lie, of course. She actually loved wine. But she didn't want the drink to dull her senses. She had the feeling that she was going to need her wits to make it through whatever Jacob had planned for the rest of the evening and she wanted to be able to defer whatever he had in mind.

To do that, she needed to have her head clear and full use of all her faculties.

"I am sorry to hear that. If I had known, I would have had other drinks available."

She dismissed his statement with a wave of her hand. "'Tis no' an issue. I am fine, really."

"I suppose you like the whisky I had previously dismissed."

She could drink it, but it wasn't her preference. She enjoyed champagne the best. But even if Jacob offered her the finest champagne from France, she would still deny the drink with the same excuse.

Standing by the fire, she watched as he finished his glass of wine and hastily poured himself another. Thankful he kept to his side of the room and didn't approach her.

There was a chaise in the room, its light blue fabric faded and stained. She wanted to sit but refused to sit there. Doing so she feared would seem like an invitation for Jacob to sit down beside her and that was the last thing she wanted.

After finishing his current glass, and then immediately pouring another one and downing that one as well, Jacob started getting a flush to his skin, his eyes glassing over. Clarissa had seen the telltale signs of one imbibing too much a time or two in her life. He was definitely on his way to crossing that line.

His temperament changed. He straightened his shoulders, showing a confidence in himself that he had lacked previously. He sauntered over, his strides sure and strong. The wine giving him a bravado he hadn't possessed before.

That was not the effect she was hoping for.

As he neared, she took a step back.

Clucking his tongue, he tsked. "Are you trying to run from me, Clarissa?"

"Miss Gordon," she corrected. "And nay," she lied as she retreated another step only to find the hardness of the wall at her back.

With lightning speed, he was in front of her, pressing his body against hers. She pushed against his chest, disgust making her stomach turn.

"Come now. Do not fight me. After all, this is what you agreed to." He brought his mouth down to kiss her, but she pushed against him.

"I most certainly did no' agree to such a thing."

"You did. And if you want those damned sheep to live, you will."

Her heart skipped in her chest. She would not allow him to follow through with what he'd threatened, nor would she allow him to touch her. Reaching into her sleeve, she clasped the handle of the knife she'd tucked away there.

"Cease your advances, Baron." She pushed against him again, one last warning.

He answered her with a slap that rattled her teeth and took her by surprise. With her free hand she clasped her cheek with a cry, her skin burning. That was the only time he would be touching her. As he came at her again, she raised her hand holding the knife and slashed out, catching him on his cheek. A trail of blood formed, and he cursed.

"You bitch!" Smacking the knife out of her hand, she yelped as it clattered to the floor.

She turned to run, and he caught hold of her hair, pulling her back to him.

At that moment, a loud crash sounded.

"Clarissa!"

It was Alexander. He'd come after her!

He rushed through the door, Nicholas, Gunn, Finlay, and Malcolm following on his heels. She nearly fainted in relief.

"If ye want to live to see another day, I suggest ye let the lass go, Kitt," Alexander growled, his dark eyes black as he glared at Jacob.

"What the hell are you doing here? Did you kick down my door, you bastard?"

"I am no' going to tell ye again."

Shoving her from behind, she stumbled forward, her arms pinwheeling out to steady herself. Alexander caught her in his arms. "Are ye all right, lass?" He asked, concern furrowing his brow as he studied her.

"I am fine."

His eyes paused on her cheek, and he lifted his hand to caress her skin.

She winced and Alexander's eyes flared, snapping to Jacob. Cupping his face, she drew his head to hers. "I really am fine. He is hurt worse than I," she said with a smirk.

"Ye scared me half to death, lass. Dinna e'er do that again." He crushed his mouth to hers and she melted into his arms. She didn't care that Nicholas was here and that he disapproved of a match between them. She loved this man. No matter what her brother said, it wouldn't change that.

Winding her arms around Alexander's neck, she drew him in closer. His tongue sought entry and she parted her lips, their tongues meeting and doing a decadent dance that left her gasping for breath when they finally broke the kiss.

Her skin felt heated, and her stomach was doing flip flops. He rested his forehead on hers and whispered, "I want naught but to continue this, but there is an issue I must attend to." He nodded in Jacob's direction. "Are ye sure ye arena hurt?" He rubbed his hands up and down her arms as he looked over her, making sure she really was okay.

"I really am," she stated. "Truly. I think I defended myself well." She smiled and stepped away from him, joining her brother, who, surprisingly, didn't appear to be angry with what had just transpired between her and Alexander. She walked into his open arms, and he hugged her, placing a kiss on top of her head.

"I am glad we got here in time."

"Me, too, brother."

"Ye fought." It wasn't a question.

"I did. Did ye think I wouldna?"

He smiled. "Nay. I had no doubt."

They focused their attention on Alexander and Jacob, who was cowering in a corner as Alexander rounded on him.

"Ye realize ye just attacked the Duke of Gordon's sister? He could have your head for that."

"She came here willingly," Jacob answered, his chin jutted out, but he didn't appear as strong as when it was just the two of them. He seemed to wilt under Alexander's scrutiny.

"Mayhap. But no' to be abused," he growled.

"I did no such thing."

In a flash, Alexander smashed his fist into Jacob's jaw, sending him into the wall as he tried to catch his balance.

Gunn and Malcolm stepped forward. Gunn put a hand on Alexander's shoulder. "Easy, brother."

"You fucking hit me!" Jacob sputtered, turning his head and spitting blood.

"Aye. How does it feel, seeing how ye hit the lass? Ye deserve a hell of a lot more than a single punch."

"The bitch stabbed me!"

Alexander lunged forward but was quickly held back by Gunn. "Think on this, Alexander. Be smart."

Shrugging off the hands holding him back, he rolled his head from side to side to ease the tension that had gathered in his shoulders.

He took a deep breath. Clarissa was safe. She may have a bruise in the morn where she had been clearly hit, but the wound she had inflicted on Kitt was worse. He couldn't help but smile. She had fought back. A true spitfire, she was so strong. He couldn't be more proud.

But he had to deal with Kitt.

"Do ye ken what will happen to ye when the authorities find out ye assaulted the duke's sister? Ye will be locked away."

Kitt's eyes widened, but Alexander wasn't done.

"Any standing ye thought ye would be gaining in society will be lost. Do ye truly think anyone will be looking to marry their daughter off to ye? Look around ye. Ye have no money. Just a crumbling estate. Which will wither away while ye rot in prison."

"I cannot go back to prison."

That caught Alexander's attention. "Pardon?"

"What do you want? I would prefer to leave the authorities out of this."

"I want ye to leave. Leave Scotland and go back to the states. Do that, and what transpired here today will ne'er leave this room. But if I e'er see your face again or hear that ye are back I will have your arse locked up with such haste ye willna ken what hit ye."

Alexander took a step back and watched as the emotions rolled over Kitt's weaselly face, weighing his options.

Kitt looked around the room and Alexander could tell the moment the bastard realized he was out of options.

"I agree to your terms. I will make arrangements to leave first thing in the morn. I never liked this damn country in the first place. You all are a bunch of barbarians."

Alexander cocked an eyebrow in his direction. "Ye havena left yet. I would choose your words wisely whilst we are still here."

"Take Clarissa home, Alexander." Malcolm stepped forward. "I will stay with Baron Kitt here and ensure he follows through with your agreement."

"As will I," Gunn chimed in.

Kitt's eyes widened as Gunn crossed his arms and glared at him.

"Thank ye, brothers." With a last look to Kitt, he spun on his heel and approached Clarissa who still stood with Nicholas, his hands resting on her shoulders.

"Go ahead," Nicholas whispered. "I see it now. And I willna be the one to stand in your way."

Clarissa spun around and clasped her brother in a tight hug. "Thank ye, brother." She kissed him on the cheek before turning to Alexander.

He opened his arms, and without hesitation, she ran into them, her body molding to his in the perfect fit. He met Nicholas's gaze. 'Thank ye,' he mouthed.

Nicholas gave him a curt nod before turning and stepping outside, Finlay on his heels.

"How about we go home?"

"To your home?"

"Nay, lass. To *our* home."

"I like the sound of that."

A smile on his face, he placed his hand at the small of her back and led her outside. "If ye like the sound of that, how do ye like the sound of Duchess of Argyll?"

She paused just outside the door and spun to him. "Are ye..." she let the question go unfinished, hanging in the air.

"Aye, I am."

The smile on her face was bright enough to lighten the darkest of days. She jumped into his arms, wrapping her legs around his waist and hugging him close. "I love the sound of that."

"Och, but lass?"

She pulled back to meet his gaze. "Aye?"

"Remind me ne'er to make ye mad."

The sound of her laughter was music to his ears.

A FEW DAYS later, Alexander oversaw the return of his flock. The Campbell sheep were back where they belonged—on his land, grazing in his fields.

Malcolm and Gunn had returned this afternoon to say that Kitt had secured travel back to the states. After delivering the news, his friends left to return to their homes. He couldn't thank them both enough for all they had done to help. Alexander was curious about what type of legal troubles he had gotten himself into in the past. They were bad enough that he had already served time in prison. Whether that was here in Scotland or in the states, he had no idea. Most likely it was in the states. But none of that mattered now that Kitt was gone. He didn't expect to ever lay eyes on the louse again.

"What are ye thinking about?" Clarissa came up from behind

him, wrapping her arms around his waist.

He turned, kissing her forehead. "Nothing of importance now that ye are here." Holding her close, with her head resting on his chest, warmth filled him.

"They look so happy," she said, nodding towards the sheep. "'Tis as if they ken they are home."

"Aye. I suppose they do in a sense. The land is familiar to them."

"Hmm."

Her sigh vibrated through him. Content filled him. He could stand here holding Clarissa in his arms for the rest of his days and he would want for naught. Everything he ever wished for was right here, with her arms looped around his waist.

She looked up at him, her chocolate brown eyes searching. "Ye seem quiet today. Is something amiss?"

"Nay," he shook his head, a smile lifting the corners of his mouth. "E'rything is perfect."

Dipping his head, he captured her mouth in a searing kiss, and she melted in his arms. He lost himself in her kisses, but as his body roared to life, he longed for more. Hands roaming the length of her back, they settled on her buttocks, and he couldn't stop the urge to pull her forward. To bring her against his hardened length.

His want for her was all consuming.

Clarissa broke the kiss and gazed at him with rounded eyes, but she didn't back away from his touch. Nay, instead the wee minx gave him a devilish smile and pushed closer to him.

"Lass, ye are going to be the death of me." He took a small step back, his body instantly missing the contact. "Ye brother will kill me if he sees this."

"He willna. He and Gwen left a bit ago." She pulled him in closer. "They will be gone for quite some time." Stepping up on tiptoes, she tipped her head up to his.

All control thrown to the wind, she yelped as he scooped her up in his arms and carried her into the house, up the stairs and into his bedchamber, kicking the door closed behind them.

As he set her down, she reached out to the nearby wardrobe and steadied herself, her beautiful eyes focused on him.

The vision of her standing there, in his room, before him, was a straight shot to his groin and his body roared to life. What was he doing?

"We canna do this."

Confusion marred Clarissa's gorgeous face. "I dinna understand."

"Och, lass. I want ye. With all my being I want ye. I have ne'er yearned for something as I do for ye."

She stepped closer. "I feel the same. We are to be married. Is that no' enough?"

He threw his head back and barked out a laugh. "Ye truly are going to be the death of me. We arena wed yet. We must wait." He couldn't believe the words as they left his mouth. That was how he kenned Clarissa was his match. She was the only woman that could make him do the right thing.

And he loved her for it.

CHAPTER TWENTY

THREE WEEKS LATER, after the fastest wedding planning that Alexander had ever seen, Clarissa stood before him, now his wife. The ceremony took place at Inveraray Castle with all of their families and friends in attendance. Though Christopher did not make an appearance.

"So, Your Grace," Clarissa drawled as she sidled up to him. "The guests have left or are tucked away in their rooms." She bit her lips suggestively as she swayed from side to side. "Whatever shall we do now?"

His cock strained against his breeches.

"I told ye no' to call me that." He nipped at her lips, and she giggled as he captured her in his arms.

"Aye. I remember." She kissed his lips. "But I love how ye react when I do."

Growling, he swept her into a kiss, picking her up and moving to the bed.

"Put me down!" She swatted at this chest with a giggle.

Immediately, he acquiesced. "Sorry, lass. I didna mean to frighten ye."

She rolled her eyes. "Dinna be daft." She turned and gave him her back. "I need ye to unbutton my gown," she said over her shoulder.

"Ye dinna need to tell me twice, lass." His fingers deftly worked the buttons. Goose pimples broke out on her skin as he eased the ivory satin off her shoulders and let the material pool around her feet on the floor. Dropping to his knees, he clasped her left ankle and lifted it, slipping her low-heeled shoe off and then repeating the gesture on the right. She used his shoulders to keep her balance and he savored the way her fingers dug into his skin.

He couldn't wait to feel her nails score his back as he worshipped her body. Her skin was soft under his lips as he kissed his way up her inner leg. He smiled at her sharp intake of breath. Purposely, as hard as it was, and as much as his body wanted him to, he ignored the juncture of her thighs and continued kissing his way back up her body, dragging her chemise with him as he went, before pulling it over her head and letting it fall to the floor.

A hiss escaped his lips at the epitome of perfection standing naked before him. "Ye are beautiful, lass."

Her cheeks flushed pink as her teeth worried her lower lip and she looked at him through her long lashes.

"I am a blessed man to be able to call ye my wife."

She looped her arms around his neck, pressing herself against him. "I feel I am the one blessed." She kissed his neck, sending a shiver straight to his cock and he groaned. "I get ye as my husband." She kissed him again. "Nicholas no longer wants to wring your neck, which is a positive thing," she giggled against his neck. "Make me your wife in every possible way, Your Grace," she purred, lying onto the bed.

He feasted his eyes on the delectable minx before him and made quick work of his clothes. Pride burst through him as her eyes settled on his manhood and widened.

His body covering hers, the heat between them rivaled the rays of the sun on the warmest day. Clarissa sighed, her hardened nipples pressing into his chest. Taking her breasts into his hands, he massaged the soft globes that fit perfectly into his palms. He suckled on a stiff peak, drawing it into his mouth.

Arching off the bed, she pushed her breast further into his mouth and savored it as if it was his last meal on earth. He moved to the other breast and lavished it with the same attention.

Her chest heaved. "Ye like that?" he asked wickedly, already knowing her answer.

"Och, aye," she sighed. "Verra much."

With a raised brow he watched her face's reaction as he kissed his way down the valley between her breasts, lower, placing kisses on her ribs before continuing even lower. He paused at her navel, darting his tongue out and she gasped.

When he settled himself between her thighs, her sex so close he could smell the sweet scent of her, he couldn't wait to taste her. With a flick of his tongue, he touched the sensitive nub and she nearly jumped off the bed.

Chuckling against her, he put an arm across her stomach to keep her still. Dragging his tongue along her soft folds, he savored her essence. Her hips bucked with such force as he continued licking, he had to add more pressure with his arm. Incomprehensible sounds escaped from her throat. When he pushed in a finger, working it in and out, she writhed, her heels digging into the mattress. He added another finger, readying her to take him.

His cock was painfully hard, and all Alexander could think about was burying himself deep within her. But he couldn't rush her. He wanted to make this as pleasurable for her as possible. So, he took his time. Her body clamped down on his fingers, and her legs began to stiffen. He sucked her sensitive nub into his mouth and rolled his tongue around it.

With a scream, she cried out. He kept stroking his fingers in and out until her legs loosened and her chest heaved.

Moving up her body, he brought his mouth down to hers and kissed her deeply. Knowing that she could taste herself on his tongue made him harder than he thought possible. Positioned at her opening, he pushed slightly.

Wide eyes bore into his and she gasped.

"I'm sorry, love. This will hurt, but only for a moment."

She nodded, her fingers twirling strands of hair at his neck. "I ken. But I am ready."

"Are ye certain?"

"Aye."

He brought his hand down between them and his thumb found her sensitive spot and he rubbed lazy circles, kissing her neck, her breasts, until her body flared to life beneath him. Just as she was about to tumble over the edge once again, he pushed forward, breaking the barrier and quickly stilled at her sharp intake of breath.

Capturing her lips in a deep kiss, he attempted to take her mind off the pain, and waited for her to be ready to continue.

His body wanted to forge ahead. She was so tight and soft around his cock. The wait was torturous.

She shifted her hips, and he broke the kiss. Tears were in the corner of her eyes, and he kissed them away.

"I wish I could have taken that pain in your place, lass. Are ye well?"

Moving her hips again, she tested her feelings, and nodded. "Make me your wife, Your Grace."

He growled and nipped at her neck, withdrawing his cock before pushing slowly back in. They found their rhythm and soon he was lost in her body. His hips worked of their own accord. He took her bent leg and wrapped it around his waist. She yelped at the sensations the new position offered.

He felt his own body tighten, knew he was getting close. He pumped his hips harder. Clarissa met each thrust, her nails scoring his back sent him over the edge. With a growl, he emptied his seed into her. One final thrust and he collapsed onto the bed beside her, pulling her on top of him.

With strong fingers, he swept her hair out of her flushed face. "Ye are amazing." He kissed the tip of her nose and she giggled.

"Thank ye for being so gentle."

"I fear I wasna as gentle as I could have been towards the end," he confessed.

"Ye were perfect. I liked it verra much."

"Did ye?"

"Aye," she smiled, a wicked glint gleaming in her eyes.

"When can we do that again?"

He barked out a laugh, making her bounce on top of him. "In due time, lass. I need a few moments first."

The rest of the night was spent keeping his promise.

IN THE MORNING, Clarissa awoke sore, but sated as she had never been. Alexander had proven to be a gentle and caring lover. Instructional as well. She had learned things she couldn't have imagined. And she wanted to do it all over again.

Alexander slept soundly beside her, and she watched him as his chest rose and fell with each breath. She took the time to admire his strong body. His broad shoulders and expansive chest, with just a sprinkling of hair. The muscles of his stomach showed that he remained active and took care of himself. The vee of his hips had her blushing.

She wanted to trail her fingers down the dusting of hair that led from his navel, and lower.

"Ye look ready to feast as if ye've been starving," Alexander said, his voice low, and she met his eyes. "Come here." He pulled her on top of him and lifted his hips.

His hardness poked her belly and wetness pooled between her thighs.

"Straddle me, love."

She looked at him questioningly, unsure what he meant.

Helping her to maneuver her legs to each side of him, she felt his cock at her opening and sank down onto it, filling her to the hilt. She sighed as pleasure washed over her.

"Now lift and drop back down," he instructed through his clenched jaw.

The movement felt awkward at first, but once she found her rhythm, the feeling was amazing. Wickedly delightful. And seeing the emotions play on Alexander's face, knowing she had the power to elicit such reactions from him gave her a sense of power she was unaware she had.

He sat up, sucking a taut nipple into his mouth as he began to pump his hips up. Her stomach tightened; the feeling now familiar, she savored it. Ready to ride the wave as it consumed her. With a cry, she called his name and when she tumbled over the edge into oblivion, Alexander followed.

"I love ye, lass," he said when she collapsed onto his heaving chest.

She smiled, kissing the soft hairs, reveling in his soft gasps.

Everything she dared dream had come true. Happiness enveloped her. She couldn't wait to see what their future held.

EPILOGUE

Three months later

ALEXANDER LOOKED AT Clarissa, concern creasing his brows. "I am going to call for the doctor. Ye have done this for a week now. Ye canna keep anything down."

She smiled at his worry. He had not put two and two together to figure out what her *illness* meant. "That willna be necessary."

"Ye canna go on like this. Ye will wilt away to naught." He pushed his hands through his dark hair the way he always did when he was worried.

They were back at Millwool. The sheep had been sheared and they were checking on the wool production. Alexander, not needing the loan from the bank, had denied their offer and Kitt was a distant memory. No word from Christopher had arrived yet, but they both hoped that he fared well.

"I insist ye see the doctor," Alexander continued, his eyes pleading.

"Your Grace," she laughed as his eyes flared, and she ignored him. She loved teasing him. He got so perturbed. "There is no need for a visit. 'Tis normal behavior for my condition."

"Your condi—" the words trailed off as recognition dawned on his face. "Ye, ye are with child?" he asked, falling to his knees in front of her, his palms splayed over her still flat stomach.

"Aye." Tears sprouted in her eyes at his reaction.

He kissed her stomach before getting to his feet and enveloping her in a hug. "I am the luckiest man alive. Do ye ken that? Ye have made me so happy. But now ye are most definitely seeing the doctor. Prepare to be pampered. In fact," he looked frantically around the room, his eyes settling on the chair. He grabbed it and dragged it over to where she stood. "Sit. Ye should no' be on your feet."

She laughed. "I am fine. Truly, I am."

He captured her mouth in a kiss. "I love ye with all my being."

"And I ye." She clasped his hand and pulled. "Now, come. I hear a carriage approaching."

In the courtyard, Clarissa impatiently waited for the carriage to come to a stop. When the door opened, and Gwen exited, belly round with her own bairn, she squealed and ran to her for a hug.

She couldn't wait to break the happy news to Gwen and Nicholas.

The cousins, due to be born only a few months apart, would be the first in what she hoped would be many children for both of them.

Alexander hugged her from behind, his hands splayed on her belly as he kissed her neck.

"I love ye, lass.

"And I love ye, Your Grace."

He growled close to her ear. Her new favorite sound.

ABOUT THE AUTHOR

Award-winning author Brenna Ash is addicted to coffee, chocolate, and all things Scotland and BTS. She's a firm believer that one can never have too much purple or glitter. She loves rom-cons and always cries at the HEAs.

When she's not busy writing about sexy, Scottish Highlanders, Medieval Pirates, Regency Rogues, or co-hosting the true crime podcast, Crime Feast, she spends her time reading with her favorite music playing in the background, binge-watching Outlander and Bridgerton, park-hopping with her besties, spoiling her cat, Lilly, or watching BTS content online. Brenna lives with her husband on the Space Coast in sunny Florida.

Website – www.brennaash.com
Amazon – amazon.com/stores/author/B01H46ZA02
Facebook – facebook.com/BrennaAshAuthor
Instagram – instagram.com/brennaashauthor
BookBub – bookbub.com/profile/brenna-ash

9 781963 585698